MW01139456

i

Time
Burrito

By

Aaron Frale

With great burrito comes great responsibility

Contents

To the memory of Digby Wolfe, a mentor and friend.

1

Chef Andre Pierre Jaramillo, or Pete for short, wanted to make the perfect breakfast burrito because his life was a mess. His food truck was a derelict crap factory that a cat had pissed on the day after his grand opening. He never could get the smell away. The students of the University of New Mexico bought his burritos not because they were good, but because they could get one for a dollar. If they could ignore the urine smell, they could feast for pocket change.

If he could make the perfect burrito, he could charge more. If he could charge more, maybe he could buy a storefront and get out of the university area. Pete envisioned himself making breakfast burritos for the Albuquerque mayor, shaking his hand, taking a picture, and framing it on the wall with all the other celebrities. Instead, he was listening to some ungrateful dweeb complain about a buck burrito, "There's bone in my meat."

"It's cartilage, not bone," Pete said as he changed out some wilted lettuce for slightly less wilted lettuce.

"I could have choked!" The student slammed the floppy burrito onto the counter. The other students behind him in line rolled their eyes. The piece of "bone" was no bigger than a pencil tip. It wasn't Pete's fault they tossed the entire damn cow into the grinder, and a piece of cartilage had gotten through.

"Even a baby couldn't choke on that."

"I'm going to report you. This is unsanitary. What's your permit number?"

"Sorry," Pete addressed the line of students. "We're closed!"

He slammed down the shutter to the food truck, and the angry student was drowned out by the thick metal crash. Pete slumped to the ground and pulled off a hat from his head. The front pictured a burrito. Embroidered on the back were the words: "The perfect burrito."

———

Later that evening, Pete locked up his food truck. It was November, and the days were getting shorter. It was dark by the time the dinner rush was over. He cleaned the truck and prepped for the next day. He would have had to wake at three in the morning if he were to prepare for the breakfast burrito rush, so he'd rather do it at night. By the time he was walking towards his truck, most of the students had gone home. Even the ducks at the duck pond were sleeping.

He hefted his way across campus, sucking in breath while he walked. His doctor had said he was pre-diabetic a couple of years ago. He hadn't done anything about his health and had even gained fifty pounds since the diagnosis, so he was sure he was full-blown diabetic by now—not that he cared—Pete was always walking one step closer to death.

He crossed Lomas towards the squat, brown, adobe-style Physics building. There was a lot behind the labs where he parked his truck. It was one of the most expensive lots, but he didn't see any other way he'd have time in the morning to park the trailer, the truck, and open at 7 am. At least, not if he wanted to sleep.

He'd circled the building as far as the other side when he saw a blue flash of light come from one of the windows. A loud explosion quickly followed. Pete ducked and stumbled backward. He toppled over and cracked his tailbone on the pavement.

"What the—" he yelped and pushed himself up. Before he could figure out what had happened, a man in a button-up shirt and slacks stumbled out from one of the doors of the Physics building. The man's hair was burnt, and his hands were bloody and charred. He looked at Pete and collapsed.

"Hey," Pete yelled and ran to the man. "Hey, mister. You OK?"

It was a stupid question. The man was clearly not OK. In fact, the man might have even been dead. When Pete got close enough, he poked the dude with his foot. The guy looked up and said, "It worked!"

"What? What worked?" Pete asked.

"The perfect—The perfect—" The man coughed and hacked.

"Burrito? The Perfect Burrito?"

"The perfect quantum tunneling—." The man gagged and continued. "Tell my lab assistant—that I love her."

The man died in Pete's arms. Pete stumbled backward. He was in serious trouble now. This guy was a professor, from the looks of his graying hair, and crow's feet around the outer corners of his eyes. He didn't look like any customer of Pete's. The only people who would eat his swill were college students. He'd tried to cook at the state fair once, and they'd put his truck right next to the Garduno's tent. He couldn't compete with Garduno's.

To make matters worse, there were already rumors about his burritos. Students would say they were chupacabra ground up with rat. Seniors dared freshman to eat his burritos. Frats used his burritos for pledges and pranks. He didn't care, for the most part, because it was good for business. The only reason he survived was that they were cheap. Students shoved anything in their mouth that cost a dollar. He'd tried raising the price to a buck fifty once and had lost half his business in one day.

If Pete were found by the campus police next to a dead professor, the rumors would end him. He was having enough trouble as it was. The one bedroom roach motel he called home was already one month late on rent and perpetually three months late on power. Each bill came with a friendly threatening notice that they would shut off his lights. He was seriously considering sleeping in the food truck.

He was about to run when he looked at the open door to the physics lab. He thought about what the man had said about his assistant. Maybe she was still in there. Maybe she was unconscious, or something. Maybe the lab was on fire. He imagined carrying her heroically out of the building. The *Albuquerque Journal* would say the next day, "Pete 'The Burrito Man' Jaramillo Saves Local Woman."

Pete sucked in his breath and went into the building. Smoke filled the hallway. There was a lab down the way with a door hanging off its hinges. Pete gagged and coughed. Holding his breath was much harder than it looked in the movies.

He bumbled through the hallway to the lab doorway. A network of supercomputers was on fire. In the center of the room was a long black table that reminded Pete of this busted air hockey table, with all the white paint stripped off, that his uncle Ricardo had in the basement. Except that this wasn't an air hockey table. There was some weird blue and white, glowing, crackling portal on top.

It looked like the special effects he saw in the Wayne's World movies, or was that Bill and Ted? He couldn't remember. He knew it was the one with that guy from The Matrix. Behind the table, he saw the lab assistant. She had a cute round face, brown hair, and thick black glasses. She was the most beautiful chick he'd ever seen—and he was around college students all day.

He circled the table and poked her with his feet. There would be no use saving her if she were dead. However, she stirred and mumbled something. He attempted to bend down to pick her up, but he wasn't so good at bending anymore. The extra pounds and the relatively sedentary lifestyle had taken a toll on him.

He finally maneuvered himself in a way that he could grab her by the arms. He hoisted her up and dragged her toward the doorway. Her white lab coat got stuck on the edge of the black table. He huffed and grunted but couldn't free her by force alone.

He plopped her on the ground and waddled towards the table. He leaned on the edge with one hand and went to fiddle with the lab coat with the other. His weight was too much for the table to bear. The leg cracked and shattered, sending both Pete and the science experiment to the ground.

The strange glowing portal crackled and flashed. The whirlwind of activity increased. It began to suck everything in the room towards it. Lab equipment and office supplies flew into the portal. Lightning flashed with each hungry gulp. The unconscious lab assistant started sliding towards the ravenous hole.

Pete grabbed onto her leg with one hand and onto the base of a server rack with the other. The phenomenon intensified. It swirled and engulfed everything that wasn't nailed down. Pete and the assistant rose off the ground as it ate. At the peak, Pete felt what it must have felt like to be hanging on for dear life while being sucked from an airlock.

His hand was numb, and it slipped. Pete and the lab assistant flew into the portal, and they disappeared from the room.

––––––––––

Pete woke up in the blazing hot desert sun. He spat dirt and grit from his mouth. He looked towards the Sandia mountain range that was pressed up against the side of Albuquerque, and it was right where it always had been. However, Albuquerque wasn't where it was supposed to be. There was no city whatsoever. The desert surrounded him. There were no buildings, no university, and no physics lab.

The lab assistant groaned from beyond a bush a couple of feet away. Pete ran towards her and kicked a notebook in the sand. It looked like some crazy math stuff. There were also some office supplies littering the desert. He picked up the notebook and was going for a pen when he felt the tip of a spear poke into his back followed by a loud grunt.

Pete put up his hands and turned around, dropping the notebook back into the sand. When he finally saw who was holding the spear, he thought that he was back at a Metallica concert after he had taken something his friend Tito called an "herbal supplement." It was way back when the band all had long hair. He remembered hearing the primal music and watching James Hetfield scream into the mic.

He realized, at that moment, that humans had evolved from apes. His whole life, his father had never believed it because he thought the planet was six thousand years old. Pete saw it for himself. James Hetfield melted into some sort of ape-man. Kirk went next. Thousands of years of evolution right before his eyes, and the vision all went away when some crazy screaming skinhead guy head-butted Pete and jumped back into the mosh pit.

Unlike the vision at the concert, the man in front of him was a real-life caveman. He had a large forehead, a mop of hair, and was wearing pelts. The man eyed Pete cautiously and picked up the journal. He sniffed it and took a bite. It didn't taste good, so he tossed it.

Pete went to pick up the notebook; the caveman squealed and shook his spear. Before the Missing Link was able to impale Pete, the lab assistant crawled out of a bush. She cursed and swore, "That stupid git. He thinks that he can take advantage of me. Just because I'm a woman in physics doesn't mean I'll sleep with him for a Ph.D. I'm going to report him to the provost."

Her accent made her even hotter. Pete knew it was Downton Abbey that she was speaking or was it Downtown? He wasn't quite sure where it was from. He was pretty sure Downtown Abbey was in Australia. That hot actress from Once Upon a Time was also from Australia, so he was pretty sure Downtown Abbey also happened there too. One time his friend Tito had caught him watching Downtown Abbey, and he'd had to punch his buddy so he would shut up about it.

The caveman's eyes lit up when he saw her. He let out a soft grunt, and his hold on his spear went limp. Pete used the moment to snatch up the notebook. The assistant felt around on the dirt for her glasses. They were thick hipster glasses that were almost too big for her face.

"What's this, then?" she said when she saw the two shapes of people staring at her. She was used to people staring, mostly men. It was no wonder why she wanted to lock herself up in a lab the rest of her life. She hated dealing with people. Once she found her glasses, she put them on and said, "Are you kidding me?"

She walked up to the caveman and examined him. She poked and prodded, even sniffed his hide. While she worked, she just talked to no one in particular, "The old goat knew what he was talking about. I thought he was just a pervert trying to impress his grad student. But this—a real life Homo Neanderthalensis—this is amazing, and would you look at the jawline? Completely different from the speculated—who the bloody hell are you?"

She noticed Pete for the first time. He shrugged, and said, "I'm nobody—I guess—but Pete's my name."

He stuck out his hand.

"Clara, and if you make a Doctor Who reference, I'll kill you." She stuck out her hand. However, before they were about to shake, the caveman screamed. He roared and pushed Pete to the ground. He grabbed Clara and slung her over his shoulders. Before Pete could get back to his feet, the caveman was halfway up the rise heading towards the mountains.

2

Pete ran up the hillside, huffing and puffing. The characters in Lord of the Rings made it look really easy to run for hours. The last time Pete had run was when his gym teacher had made him do it in high school. He'd had to run a whole mile, and it took him fourteen minutes, but he still beat the kid in the wheelchair.

The foothills leading to the Sandia Mountains were gigantic. He'd never realized how much so until he had to run up them himself. He stopped and puked several times during the journey, and one time he had to sit and cool off under a piñon tree. The caveman was way more physically fit than Pete, so he was long gone before Pete could crest the first hill.

However, Pete reckoned that he was smarter. He'd taken half a college class called Introduction to College Studies. He bet the caveman didn't have any college experience. So he would have to use his wits against the caveman's brawn. It was an age-old tale. Like David and Goliath. Pete was pretty sure David had challenged Goliath to a checkers match and won by outsmarting him.

Pete figured he would do the same, except he would challenge the caveman to a game of PvP in Halo. Pete was pretty good at Xbox, so he figured he could win Clara's freedom back. Now all he needed was to find them.

Lucky for Pete, he'd spent a lot of his high school years finding new places to take Tito's herbal supplements. Since he'd spent most hours after school with Tito and friends, Pete had driven all over Albuquerque and the surrounding area. There was a cave way in the mountains near Placitas that was called the Sandia Man Cave. It was a spot where archeologists had found some caveman's bones.

In Pete's time, the cave was nothing more than a place for teenagers to party. If a person went to the very back of the cave, they'd find nothing but beer bottles and graffiti. Pete and his friends had set out to party in the cave once but had found out that they would have had to walk far away from the parking lot, and had decided to hang out in the car instead.

The landscape receded from the desert into the forested foothills. Day turned to night, and after an eternity of pseudo-running, mostly walking, Pete came to a stream that he knew led to the place where the Sandia Man Cave was located. He drank from the stream greedily. He was dehydrated from his day in the sun, and the cool water was the best he had ever had.

He pulled out an empty flask of whiskey that he had used to keep himself sane while making burritos. He filled the flask and shoved it into his pocket. On the way to the cave, he drank and filled it several more times.

In his time, there had been a dirt road leading through the mountain valley. Now back in the caveman days, it was nothing more than a game trail following a riverbed. It was peaceful, back in the olden times. He never heard a car, a plane, or anything. Even when camping in the Jemez Mountains with his buddies, he would hear an occasional plane fly overhead.

The woods were dark, and the shadows were long at night. All the mysterious sounds of the forest at the witching hour seemed louder in the crisp night air. Most people would be scared of aliens or wendigos, or some crazy beasts in the woods after dark. Pete, on the other hand, liked it. He liked hearing the chirping of insects and hooting of owls. The night was always his time. He had planned to hire someone for the morning shift, as soon as his burritos got famous.

Finally, after a day and a good part of a night of walking, he saw the cave. It was easy to spot because the caveman must have lit a fire. It was blazing at the cave entrance up on the cliff face. Pete sighed. The cliff face.

In Pete's time, the cave had been at the end of a trail with a spiral staircase leading to the cave entrance. With railings, stairs, and platforms, it was a rather safe tourist experience for anyone who wanted to visit. Back in the real Sandia Man times, it was a cave on a cliff face.

An experienced rock climber would have had no trouble making it to the entrance of the cave, but Pete sometimes got winded when he had to use the stairs at his ghettotastic apartment complex. There was no way he was going to make that climb. His rescue attempt was going to end in failure. Once again, he was going to make matters worse for himself and the girl.

Oh well, she would make a good Sandia Man bride. Maybe her smart genes would create whole new smart generations, and by the time he got back to his time, they'd have Star Trek technology. He was pretty sure Wesley Crusher never used the holodeck to study. A teenager with the ability to create any scenario he wanted? A few choice ones came to mind. They wouldn't have been able to take Pete out of the holodeck if he'd had one. Especially if they'd had a Halo-themed one.

Pete was about to pack it in, and find a place to sleep for the night when he saw a figure standing at the edge of the cave entrance. If he wasn't mistaken, the figure was a short female that he'd recently had the pleasure of meeting.

"Hey," he whisper-yelled. She didn't seem to hear him. "Hey! Hey! HEY!"

The last one was a bit louder than he'd intended, but it seemed to do the trick. Clara responded, "Pete? Is that you?"

"Yeah," he said. "I'm here to rescue you!"

"I do appreciate it, but I don't need rescuing."

"Huh? I thought he was going to—um—mate with you."

"Oh, yeah. I thought so too at first, but he's been a perfect gentleman."

"He has?"

"Well, yeah, by his standards; he's attempted to pick the lice out of my hair, offered me a dead squirrel, all the things you do when you like someone."

"Does that really work?"

"The dead squirrel?"

"Yeah."

"We have nuptials planned for tomorrow."

"So that's what I've been doing wrong. No chicks ever want to sleep with me."

"Are you serious?"

"Um—" Pete had been very unlucky with women his whole life. At this point, he was ready to believe anything.

"Please promise me you'll never give a girl a dead squirrel. Look, I'm not in any real danger for now, but I think he's a bit jealous of you, so I don't think you should come up here."

That was a relief. Pete didn't even need an excuse not to come up. Plus someone was jealous of him! Pete had never made anyone jealous before. That made him feel slightly more manly, in the sense that he'd never really felt manly in his whole life.

"So what do we do now? I thought I'd challenge him to a game or something to win ownership of you." Pete said.

"First off, I'm nobody's property, and second, what game could you possibly play with a Neanderthal?" she queried.

"I was thinking Halo."

"Where are you going to get a Play Station?"

"Xbox."

"Whatever. I do appreciate the sentiment, but I think the more important question is how to get us home. Did you see if anything came through the portal with us?"

"Um," Pete pulled the notebook from where he'd tucked it into his waist. "I found this notebook."

"Good! The professor's notes. That will come in handy." She turned around and peered into the cave, "I think I hear him stirring. I suggest you make yourself scarce. Here."

She tossed down a cooked carcass of an animal. By some miracle, Pete caught the morsel, despite the way he flailed wildly every time someone threw something at him. It looked like a rabbit. It was charred and covered in some sort of seasoning. He looked it over.

Clara called down to him. "It's rabbit, with a special seasoning he made. I had some earlier. It's quite good. Now, I'll find you in the morning, and get the notebook."

"Wait!" Pete said. "How will we find each other? I'll write down my phone number in this notebook."

Pete scrawled on the first page.

"Um—Pete—" Clara said.

"Yes—" Pete said and looked up after he was done writing.

"Do you see any cell towers around?"

"I heard they look like trees now. So you never know what could be a cell tower."

"You do know that we're in the Stone Age, right?"

"Like time travel?"

"Yeah."

"That's what I figured, but did they have cell phones back then? I mean I heard once they used to be made of brick."

"That's 'brick phone,' like a bulky phone."

There was a grunt from the cave, and Clara said. "I think he's waking. Hide!" She ducked back into the cave. Pete didn't wait for the caveman to discover him. He tromped through the forest until he was out of sight. He found a relatively soft spot on the ground and popped a squat.

He looked over the rabbit several times and then decided to take a bite. It was the most wonderful flavor he'd ever experienced in his life. He ate ravenously, cleaned all the bones, and sucked every last drop of seasoning.

Later, when he was picking his teeth, he realized the seasoning on the rabbit reminded him of something. It was a flavor that was with him his entire life. It was what he'd craved when he would hang out with his friends after taking Tito's herbal supplements. It was what he dreamed about at night. It was the taste of his grandmother's cooking. It was what he'd failed to achieve in his kitchen. It was the flavor of the perfect burrito.

3

Clara woke up with a stiff back, under a bug-infested hide she'd used as a blanket. Anyone who glorified time travel as some grand adventure romping through the cosmos should just die. The stiffness came from sleeping on a cave floor all night, and the red marks on her arms and legs were from the critters that no doubt lived in the animal hide. However, when the alternative was hypothermia, she'd sleep with the bugs.

She kicked the hide off of herself and searched for her glasses. She put them on and found out that her Neanderthal friend had already left the cave, to go on an early morning hunt, no doubt. The surprising part was that all her pocket items, shoes, etc. were all stacked neatly in the corner. He must have stacked them last night for her.

He was very cordial, as far as Neanderthals go, though she had never met one in her life until now. She'd just assumed, because of the bloody, violent past of humans, that their evolutionary cousins would be violent as well. She was pleased to have been wrong, especially since her time trip could have ended with one axe blow to the head.

However, celebrations weren't in order yet, because her prehistoric friend had obviously taken a romantic attraction to her, which created several problems. She preferred finishing her Ph.D., over making hunter-and-gatherer babies. She also preferred women over men. There was also the chance that he'd turn violent when she officially rejected him for mating. Her best idea involved letting the courtship extend out as much as possible, at least until they could find a way home.

Hopefully, her dumb-and-dumber companion wouldn't get his skull caved in by a rock while her unrequited-love-interest decided to step out for a hunt. The first order of business, after relieving herself, and eating the last of the leftover rabbit, involved finding her hapless friend. Luckily enough, her dad had taken her rock climbing a lot, when she was a kid. Scaling the cliff face of the cave would be the equivalent of the kiddy hill at the RockStar gym located in a repurposed warehouse on 4th Street in Albuquerque.

Her dad was an American named Stanley, and always took risks. He did all the sports that would make her "stiff upper lip British mum's heart go a-patter." Truth be told, as much as her dad liked to pick on her mum, the woman was a risk-taker too. Rebecca Raynott was such a well-known medical researcher that her father changed *his* last name, and they were the Raynotts and not the Penalmans, though Clara had always wondered whether there was more to the name change than prestige.

Either way, her mum was always away in some country with infectious disease outbreaks, and her father threw himself from planes to keep up. Clara's parents stayed in England long enough to secure their daughter's accent, but not long enough to avoid the American High School system. Sometimes Clara cursed the University of New Mexico for giving her mum such an awesome deal to persuade her to switch countries. At least Clara's dual upbringing let her be equally comfortable when it came to the nuances of language such as chips, fries, and crisps. She could alternate word choices without even thinking about it.

It was her fond memories of her birth land that had brought her back across the Pond for her undergraduate work at the University of Surrey. However, when she wanted to get her Ph.D., the University of New Mexico was a prime choice for the type of physics she wanted to study, which brought her back to her parents again. Though as a graduate student, she elected to stay on campus in her room, rather than go back to her parents.

That was the mistake that had led her to the point where she was rock climbing down a cliff without a harness in a time before medical attention was invented. If she hadn't lived on campus, she might not have taken the lousy Graduate Assistantship that had had her babysitting her pervy professor's experiment all night. Had she not allowed her pervy professor to walk her home one evening, he might never have gotten the wrong idea implanted into his mind for several weeks, and she would never have pushed him into the controls of a freaking time machine!

That was the worst part. The experiment that had brought her back might not be replicable, because she didn't know what knob, button, or keyboard combination he'd pushed. It was an experiment for which she had adjusted the parameters hundreds of times, and zero of them had produced a brilliant swirling vortex of time in the lab. Then, she slammed a touchy jerkface into the controls, and poof, an unstable phenomenon sucks crap from the room! It was her thermos that had knocked her out, on its way to the time hole.

When she got to the bottom of the cliff, she called out for Pete. She was a little worried that her cave-dwelling friend would hear her, so it was a loud whisper. When there was no return answer, she wandered deeper into the woods, following the direction she'd thought she'd seen him go last night.

After what seemed to be an inordinate amount of time spent looking for her only link to her time period, she heard a noise coming from behind, "Hey, Clara, do you have any of that rabbit?"

Clara didn't waste any time. She grabbed the man's wrist, spun him around, and applied pressure. The unknown assailant hunched over in pain and cried out. It took her a moment to realize that the man was speaking English, and no one in this time period would have spoken English.

"Pete?" she said, as she let go.

"Damn, do you fight MMA? 'Cause that seriously hurt," Pete said, as he rubbed his arm.

"You'll be fine," she said. "It's just a little self-defense, and knowledge of pressure points."

"My arm feels numb," he said, still rubbing it.

She looked down to see the makeshift bed he had made for himself. It looked like a bed a person who'd watched too many survival TV shows might make. It was a mess of leaves and forest growth, with no real design in mind. The ground looked more comfortable than his bed.

"Are you sure you didn't just sleep on it funny?" she said.

"No, ma'am. I didn't sleep much."

"I'm not a 'ma'am.' Call me Clara."

"OK, Clara."

"So how did we get stuck together, Pete? Are you a janitor for the physics building?" Normally, she didn't like to make assumptions about people, but this guy certainly didn't have the student vibe, and, well, she knew all the professors, not that this guy would have been one of them.

"You don't recognize me?"

"Can't say that I do."

"I sell burritos by the Center of the Universe sculpture. They're world-famous, you know."

"Look, I don't get to the main campus very often. I'm sure they're delightful."

"I mean, I do all right, but they're *going* to be world-famous. Believe me."

"Sure, so do you have the book?"

"Um—I don't think so. No one's written a book about my burritos yet."

"The professor's notes!"

"Oh! That book! Why didn't you say so?"

"What other book would I be talking about?"

"It can't hurt to be more specific."

He pulled the notebook from his trousers, and she grabbed it from him before she'd thought too hard about where the notebook had been. She flipped through it. At first glance, it looked as though it *could* be the world's first mathematical guide to time travel, but she needed to study it, to be sure. It was a start. She figured that if her teacher had built a time machine, he would have also built a way to get back.

"Good," she said after a bit. "This should do. Now, I need you to gather everything you can find from the wreckage and bring it back here. I'll study the book, and figure out if I can get us home."

"Um—OK, but I need you to do something for me," he said, and grinned. Oh, here it comes. All men were the same, and she would have sworn off of them long ago if she weren't biologically attracted to females. "I need you to figure out how he makes the seasoning for the rabbit."

"What?" she said, taken aback.

"Look, it's not as if he's ever going to start a business with it. Think of it as quip pro quo."

"That's quid pro quo. It's not as if we're exchanging "yo mamma" jokes, or anything."

"OK, whatever, all I need you to do is figure out the recipe."

"I'm trying to get us home. I don't have time to help you nick a forty-thousand-year-old burrito seasoning."

"It's cultural studies! You're saying we shouldn't learn about culture when we have this amazing opportunity."

"Look, if you want to make some profit from time travel, that's your ethical dilemma, not mine. However, if it will make you get the equipment from the wreckage, I'll see what I can find out. I'm not going to measure portions. I'll just let you know what I see when he mixes it."

"You'd do that for me? You're the most awesome woman in the world."

"OK, whoa, yeah—let's focus more on the task at hand."

"Right, so how am I going to get the equipment here? That's too many trips for even me to handle, and I walk the campus every day."

"You're a modern human. Figure it out. Build a wagon. I don't care."

"The wagon sounds like a good idea. Hey, do you think cavemen have used wheel shops?"

Clara rolled her eyes and dropped her head. She was already getting a migraine just from talking to the guy. Why did she travel back before the invention of Tylenol?

4

Pete huffed, and puffed, while he dragged a makeshift wagon up a hill. It was made of several branches, strung together with twine. The wheels were tree stumps, with a hole poked in the middle, for the axle. The wagon was filled to the brim with twenty-first-century gizmos and electronics. Anything he could find was stuffed into the prehistoric hauling device.

Clara had given him pretty simple directions for what he needed to gather. "We can't leave anything behind," she had said one day, while she was carving a hole in one of the wheels. It was good to have her around because he wouldn't have known how to make a wagon. At first, he'd thought it would be easy; he'd made plenty of things in Minecraft, like a tunnel with swirling bricks that looked as if it were descending into hell. He'd used to run his character back and forth in the tunnel when he was taking herbal supplements.

When Clara saw him snapping a twig while trying to bend it around another twig, she showed him how to find and make twine. Her dad had used to camp with her in the mountains, so she knew all this survival stuff. It was super useful because Pete was good at following directions. Like when he'd learned to cook, it was at a fast food place, so it was super easy. Microwave deflated eggs. Take anemic bacon from the warmer. Toss in some cheap potatoes. One squirt of special sauce, and bam! One breakfast burrito. It was so easy; he went into business for himself.

"Even burrito wrappers?" Pete said, unsure if the trash from a couple of burritos he'd shoveled down the night he was sucked through time were still in his pocket. He didn't find them the next day and hadn't thought about it till now.

"Especially our garbage! Can you imagine how history would change if they dug up a 40,000-year-old burrito wrapper?" Clara cringed and went into some science stuff about how bad it would be.

Pete actually could imagine how history would change, because he'd seen how it changed in Back to the Future II when Biff took the sports almanac. If archeologists uncovered burrito wrappers from olden times, they would see that Pete's Burritos was a name from the ancient days. Big fast food chains would be named Pete's Burritos before he was even born. He wouldn't be able to compete, even if he *did* uncover the secret to the perfect burrito. He'd have to call them Andre, or Pierre burritos, and he hated those names. Even worse, he might have to call them Jaramillo burritos, and he hated his father most of all.

"We are talking total time collapse," Clara finished.

"I know, Taco Bell would be serving Pete's burritos!" Pete yelped.

"Do you think about anything else?"

"Sometimes. Like, I always wondered if Robert Trujillo will be in Metallica forever, or just another bassist to pass through. Bassist in the Wind. Get it? Like Dust in the Wind but for Metallica bassists?"

"—Sometimes I fulfill my yearning for intellectual pursuits with Unk."

'Unk' was the name Clara had given to the caveman who had taken a liking to her. He was always giving her gifts of dead rabbits, and porcupine bladders. He'd even accepted Pete, once he knew they weren't competing for the same woman. Their first encounter was a little scary because Pete wasn't sure if he was going to be murdered or not.

It was on the morning two days after they'd gotten stranded in the past. Pete had gathered most of the materials for the wagon. Clara was lecturing him about twine, and Pete's mind was wandering off, thinking about this woman that he had met a few days before his adventure in time. She was like way hot, but not like Clara hot. Clara was out-of-his-league hot. His scientific friend had movie star good looks, and probably shopped at Prada, or wherever sexy people shop. The woman he liked was Walmart hot, and it was just his luck that she was trying to carry too much to her car. He offered to help and dropped her bag halfway.

So, Pete was daydreaming about what if he had made it to the car, while Clara was saying something about twine when there was a battle cry from the forest. Unk tackled Pete and pinned him under his legs. The caveman lifted a rock high in the sky. Pete thought the last thing he'd see was a grimy hand, clenching a rock, surrounded by the serene treetops, and a clear blue sky. But another pair of hands touched Unk's. Clara's light caress brought the murderous hand down.

She pulled Unk off of Pete. The caveman grabbed Clara and held her close. He beat his chest once, and grunted, "Unk."

"Yes, Unk," Clara said. "I know you're trying to protect me, but Pete's not a threat."

Pete dusted himself off, and said, "Yeah, mister. I don't want to fight anybody."

Unk tensed up when Pete stood, and Clara calmed him down.

Clara took Unk's hand and held it out. Pete took it, and weakly shook it. "Look, friends," Clara said, in a soothing voice. "Yes, that's right. Friends."

Unk gripped Pete by the forearm and squeezed tightly. Pete felt as if it were about to pop, as when he would step on an errant burrito on the floor. The caveman pulled until they were eye to eye. Pete gave a half-smile, half-grimace. Unk let go and laughed. It almost sounded like the cry of a zoo animal. The man from prehistory patted his newfound friend on the back and started laughing some more.

After that day, the caveman seemed more like a meathead frat boy best friend, than an ancient ancestor. Unk was always shoving dubious food at his modern friend to try, and when Pete's lips would pucker, the prankster would laugh and laugh that wild animal laugh. It didn't stop there. Pete would wake up cradling a porcupine, while Unk hooted with laughter. He would slip on mud placed near his peeing patch by the river. After a while, he wondered if it might be better to be an enemy of the caveman than be a friend.

Pete finally crested the hill, and all his thoughts drifted away. He sat down on a rock at the top that overlooked the landscape. He could see for miles in any direction. He wiped the sweat from his brow and gulped down water from one of Unk's waterskins. Pete made sure to sniff for the odor of urine before he sipped. Some of the pranks were a slow burn. The water was safe, and he gulped it down.

After he had been satisfied, he saw something in the distance. There were figures moving down the Rio Grande River. Pete had almost missed it. He had spent a few weeks or so in the past, and he was on his last wagon trip picking up debris from the lab. During that time, he had gotten used to the stillness of the time before technology. At first, it was unnerving, not hearing traffic or airplanes. His world was always in motion, whether it be a siren or a motorcycle. But after a few days, he liked the tranquility.

He was so used to sitting on this hill and feeling as if he were the only person on the planet, he'd almost forgotten that there were other people, and not all of them were the merry-prankster-type like Unk. He pulled out a pair of binoculars he'd found in the wreckage a couple of days ago and scanned the horizon.

On a barren patch that was surrounded by desert, rather than the Bosque, a group of cavemen followed the river. From the looks of it, they were a war party. They had axes and paint. One of the men pointed towards Pete and gesticulated wildly. They doubled their pace. Pete shoved the binoculars into his pack. He hoisted the harness he had made for the wagon. He dragged his load back to the cave as fast as he could go.

5

Pete almost died from exhaustion when he pulled the wagon to the foot of the cave's cliff. It wasn't "fake" dying-from-exhaustion either. It was real lungs-burning, legs-like-jelly, and sweating-so-much-he-didn't-have-any-more-sweat-left-type of dying. After all the times he'd "fake" died in gym class, it was a wonder his teacher, Tex, hadn't caught on.

Pete used to loathe sports, mainly because he wasn't good at them and would always embarrass himself. Tex would always yell, and say things like "Get in the game, Jaramillo!" and "Eyes on the ball, Jaramillo!" which didn't mean much to Pete, because he had poor depth perception, and would always miss the ball. Pete would always give up, and Tex would scream, "Fine! You want to go sit around and put flowers in your hair; go do it!"

Pete always figured it was because Tex hated people with long hair, and since Pete was a metal head in high school, he always had long hair. However, later on, long after the humiliations of gym class, he'd found out the truth. This Sixties, free-love, protestor guy came to his class to talk about New Mexico during the civil rights movement. He passed around this book of newspaper clippings from the *Albuquerque Journal*, and one of the headlines said, "Student at UNM Stabbed by Hippies!" The front page showed a young Tex bleeding from the gut and being shoved into an ambulance. It wasn't metal heads he hated. It was hippies!

Pete shoved the wagon onto a platform that Clara had constructed. It was a makeshift elevator, that lifted up towards the cave with a pulley system. He tugged on a rope and hoisted himself to the top. Unk looked out over the edge, grunted, and grinned. When Pete was almost at the top, the rope slipped, and he went into free-fall. He didn't react. It was part of the normal Unk antics he had come to expect. Just before hitting the ground the platform stopped, and the wild laugh echoed off the canyon walls.

After finally getting to the top, Pete tossed the wagon harness to the ground, and let out a sigh of relief. The cave was scattered with all the junk he had gathered over the last couple of weeks. Unk shoulder-chucked him and offered him a rabbit. Pete motioned for water, and Unk tossed him a water skin.

After sniffing for urine, and drinking only when he knew it was safe, Pete wandered to the back of the cave, where Clara was doing her best to reconstruct the device that had gotten them there. The device looked as if it was pretty close to the one he remembered from the lab, even though it was propped up on several rocks, rather than the sleek air-hockey-table-looking thing.

Clara didn't look back at him as she worked. She talked before he could say anything, "Most of the equipment from the lab wasn't important to time travel. It was monitoring devices to observe the phenomenon, and record everything. The good news is that the time vortex sucked up everything we needed to get home. I also have figured out a way to stabilize it, so that we can choose a specific time and day."

"What's the bad news?" Pete asked.

"Between all the battery components I could scrounge from my phone, the laboratory laptops, and so forth, I figure we have enough power for one portal."

"I have the battery on my phone." Pete offered and pulled out his phone. He had turned it off when he first arrived, to save the battery.

Clara waved her hand. "Oh, no, one cell phone battery won't add much more power than we've already got. Besides, we'll need it to hitch a ride."

"Like on a TARDIS?"

"I told you, 'If you make a Doctor Who reference, I'll kill you!' No, we won't be able to fly around with our time machine, just travel through time with it. So it will deposit us in the future at this exact spot. We'll need to hitch a ride back to town."

"So we're going back?"

"*If* I calibrated the time circuits correctly *if* it stays open long enough to get us through, but if there was something broken that I missed—what I'm saying is, that while we have a chance at getting home, it's not a very good one."

"Well, I didn't learn how Unk does the seasoning anyway," Pete said, which was true. He'd watched Unk prepare the ingredients. He'd even tried it himself, but it wasn't the same. Unk had been mixing the seasoning together his whole life. Pete was trying to do it for the first time, and it wasn't as if there were teaspoons and tablespoons to help Pete out. Unk did it all from memory and intuition. Pete knew what was in it, but couldn't get the portions right.

"Is that all you think about?" Clara said.

"Unk is a genius at work! For a caveman, he's elegant and graceful! It's like watching a ballet dancer do all the moves, and then trying them out yourself! You'd never be that good—not that I tried ballet before! Shut up! I've never worn a leotard!"

Clara put her hands up. "I didn't say you did."

"Good," Pete said. "Because that wouldn't be very manly."

"I was never questioning your manliness."

"OK! So I did it one time! Those moves were just so beautiful."

A scream erupted from the front of the cave. It was Unk, and while they had gotten to know his various grunts and communication styles during their weeks in the past, they had never heard a wail like it. It was primal and terrifying. Both Clara and Pete dropped what they were doing, and ran to the front of the cave to see what was going on.

They looked over the edge of the cliff, to the valley down below, and a rock nearly hit Clara across the head. Unk pulled her away, just in time. Pete jumped back when another rock came his way. In the brief time they were able to survey the scene, Pete noticed the war party he had seen in the distance. They were at the bottom of the ravine. Two of them had slings and were pelting the cave with rocks. The others were scaling the wall with battle axes dangling at their sides, and primitive knives clenched in their teeth.

"Oh, yeah, I forgot to mention," Pete said. "I saw a war party while I brought up the last load."

"You didn't say this earlier?" Clara said, exasperated.

"I didn't think they'd be able to follow me. I was pretty far away when they saw me. There's no way they could have seen me once I got to the woods."

"You didn't think that hunters-and-gathers could track you. Emphasis on the 'hunters' part."

"I thought that was only something they taught to Army Rangers. I saw this movie once where a guy had to find another guy in the woods—"

Another rock hit the cave ceiling, ricocheted, and almost would have hit Pete if Clara hadn't pushed him out of the way. Unk wailed and pointed to the invaders.

"Gather everything from our time period," Clara said. "I'm going to start the vortex."

Pete nodded. He began gathering all the twenty-first-century objects. Luckily enough, they were all spread out on animal hides. All Pete had to do was cinch up the hides, and tie them off. Unk saw what Pete was doing, and started to help. For all the TV shows that depicted cavemen as these grunting lunkheads, they seemed to be pretty smart. They had to be pretty smart if they were inventing tools. Pete knew what an axe was because he had grown up with them. The people of this time had to invent one.

Once all the bags of twenty-first-century goods were ready to go, they dragged them to the back of the cave. Clara was working furiously to finish up the machine. She flipped open a laptop that was hooked into the machine and turned back to Pete. "You got everything?"

"Yeah!" Pete said.

"Are you sure? If there is just one trace of our stuff left here, we could alter the future permanently."

"I'm sure. I got it all!" Pete said.

There were wails from the front of the cave. The warriors were getting close to the top. Clara turned back to the device and pressed a few keys on her laptop. The vortex ignited and sucked in all the electronics around it. Clara, Pete, and Unk began gathering all the hides full of twenty-first-century items and threw them inside.

Just as they'd tossed the last of it into the vortex, the war howl of the marauders came closer. One of the stones slung into the cave hit the ceiling, bounced off, and clunked Clara in the head. She collapsed into Pete's arm.

She said, "I'll be fine. Get the wagon!"

"But you're hurt!" Pete said.

"We can't leave anything behind. Can you imagine what would happen if we'd invented the wheel too early?"

Pete imagined a bunch of cavemen racing around in Mario-Cart-style go-carts throwing turtle shells at each other. It was kind of sweet, but she was smarter than he was, so he complied.

"Unk!" Pete said. "You take her through."

"No!" Clara said. "We can't mess with anything!"

"He'll die!"

"What if he was supposed to die?"

"I don't think they would have seen me if I hadn't been gathering parts."

"If we hadn't been here, then maybe Unk would have been out for a walk. We can go on in circles, but the truth remains, that we must do as little harm to the past as possible. This man could be the sire of all the Native American tribes in New Mexico, for all we know! There's more cave deeper into the mountain! He can hide!"

The war yowls were now at the mouth of the cave. Clara yelled, "Go! Hurry!"

Clara stumbled toward the portal. Pete dashed to the front of the cave. He saw the wagon. It was about halfway between him and the war party. The cavemen were poking through the hides, bones, and Unk's tool collection. Pete dashed for the wagon.

The warriors looked up and saw him. They ran in his direction. Despite being exhausted earlier, adrenaline kicked in, and he found the energy to cover the distance. He slipped on a wet patch on the cave floor, as an axe flew over his head, and hit the cave wall. He skidded to a halt next to the wagon.

The warriors were right on top of him. They were a snarling mass, with brutal stone weapons that resembled bludgeoning tools, more than cutting implements. The men reminded Pete of Orcs, although Pete wasn't Gimli, as much as he wanted to be. Pete rolled into the wagon and pushed himself forward. He hit the ground a couple of times to get going full speed.

Two more axes flew overhead as he rolled towards the vortex. Unk was staring at the portal in confusion. He was no doubt trying to figure out what had happened to his lost love. Seeing Unk stare dumbly at the portal gave Pete an idea. Maybe he had been going about it all wrong. For the last couple weeks, he had been trying to figure out Unk's secret to seasoning, so that he could recreate it himself.

Maybe the secret to the perfect burrito wasn't something Pete could do on his own. Any great restaurant wasn't just the product of one person. There was always a staff behind every great person. Gordon Ramsey had sous chefs, Stephen King had editors, and Metallica had that therapist who appeared in that tour video—which was kind of stupid, Pete thought. Part of what made Metallica cool was that they walked into a liquor store and didn't pay for it, and drove over the lines on roads. They were rebellious. Rebels don't need therapy!

Either way, the point was clear. The perfect burrito wasn't the creation of one man, but the collaborative effort of many. Pete could be Steve Jobs, and Unk, the Woz. It was the perfect match, and a whole lot better alternative for Unk, than if Pete were to leave him behind. How much could history change for a man who was going to die anyway?

When Pete rolled past Unk, he stuck his foot out and tripped the caveman. It was just enough to put Unk into the gravitational pull of the vortex. Unk screamed as he was sucked into it. This time, Pete got the last laugh. He chuckled to himself and was sucked into the portal, wagon and all, seconds later.

6

Clara was the first through the portal. It crackled and spat her out onto the cave floor. The previous time she had been unconscious when it thrust her forth, so she wasn't prepared for how much time travel hurt, or more accurately, how much being ejected from a portal at high speed hurt. It was no surprise that after skidding to a halt, arms protecting her skull, the first thing to come out of her lips was "Ow." She touched her head, and though there was dried blood from where the rock had struck her, at least the bleeding had stopped.

There was something 'off' about the cave. It wasn't the 40,000 or so years that had passed in the blink of a second, nor was it the lack of Unk's stuff littering the cave, that she had grown used to seeing during her stint in the past. It was something she couldn't quite wrap her mind around.

She had set the controls correctly. She'd scheduled the jump to happen a couple of hours before they had traveled in the first place. The idea behind her calculations was that if she appeared in a cave at night, people would get suspicious. At least now she could make up a story about taking the lab equipment away for field experiments. If they got to the city from the cave with enough time, she could save the professor. As much as she hated the pervy teacher, the git had discovered time travel, and he didn't deserve to die the way Pete had said he did.

Before she was able to lift herself from the place where she had landed, the portal crackled again. Unk came flying out, followed by Pete on the wagon. She rolled out of the way at the last minute, and they crashed into a pile of wood, and the other crap that had been sucked through. Unk groaned. Pete jumped up from the ground, and yelled, "That was awesome!"

"You took Unk! I told you not to take Unk!" Clara said.

"He was going to die—and trust me, when you taste the burritos we can make together—"

"He's a historical footnote! Not a co-founder! There's no telling what you've changed."

"Hey, where's all the graffiti?"

"What?"

"The graffiti," Pete said and motioned to the smooth cave walls. "There used to be graffiti all over this cave."

Clara's throat went tight. She looked around the cave walls, and they were surprisingly clean. It wasn't just tidy; it lacked dust, slime, and anything a person would expect to be in a cave. It was a shining and well-preserved example of a cave. It was almost as if they were in a museum. Clara ran towards the front.

Pete pulled Unk from the pile of wagon and time travel machine parts. "There, there, buddy. You can crash at my place tonight. I'll show you the truck in the morning—"

At the front of the cave, Clara was shocked to see that they *were* in a museum. There were life-like statues of Neanderthals in the cave. However, instead of carving stone axes and picks, they were pounding out iron weapons and wearing medieval clothing. There were women weaving baskets, and kids playing what looked like "Go." Had they not had the distinct forehead ridges, Clara could have sworn they were in some strange Western-and-Eastern-influenced hybrid history, with Neanderthals in the leading role.

The strangest part was not the life-sized tableau, but the group of Native American students gawking at Clara at the mouth of the cave on the other side of the dividing rope. They looked like a bunch of bored middle school kids in various stages of teenage development. There was one kid of European descent in the group. He had a peculiar shirt that said "Titanland 2014" on the front. The teacher's back was to Clara. She had a deep nasally voice and lectured the students. "Your ancestors used to work with iron and wove baskets. When Standing Bull sailed across the seas to Europe, the Native Europeans were just starting to craft items made of iron. By that time, the great tribes had already invented steel and gunpowder. The technology during the ensuing cultural clashes put the Native Europeans at a distinct disadvantage."

A stout and bulky Native American boy put his hand up.

"Fire Wind. Yes, do you have a question?" the teacher said.

"Is that why all Native Europeans are lazy and collect checks from their casinos all day?" Fire Wind smirked, and the class laughed.

"That is not appropriate! The colonizing force brutalized the Native Europeans—" The teacher scolded.

"That white chick doesn't seem to be brutalized." Fire Wind pointed at Clara.

Pete dragged Unk from the back of the cave. Unk still seemed out of it. The teacher turned around. She was also Native American and dressed as if she were out of a J. Crew catalog. The teacher's eyes surveyed the three people in the display case, and her hands went down to a device in her pocket. Judging from the big red button on the device, the teacher had hit a panic button. She smiled and told the kids to proceed in an orderly manner to the next exhibit.

Two security guards ran down the hall towards them. Clara didn't have time to gather the time travel device. They found themselves cuffed by the guards minutes later.

Pete felt as if he were in a Sci Fi movie wonderland. Most people would be scared of being in an unfamiliar situation, but not Pete. He was always an explorer. His parents' house was on the Westside of Albuquerque, right up where the city disappeared, and the desert seemed to go on forever. On some days when his old man would drink too much, and start looking for things to hit, Pete would jump the fence and strike out into the desert.

Among the tumbleweeds and the cacti, Pete had pretended he was an explorer like Indiana Jones, looking for arrowheads or petroglyphs. The petroglyph park wasn't all that far from Pete's house. His best friend said there were over ten thousand ancient carvings among the volcanic rock that made the West Mesa. Even though the volcanic rock was too far from his house, he'd still search, in hopes that one day he'd find some ancient Native American relic, and maybe get his name in the *Albuquerque Journal*.

Now that he was in some hidden Native American society, Pete was completely stoked. Who would have thought that a lost tribe would be so close? On what used to be the cliffside were various exhibits just like the one he was in, and on the other side, there was a long white wall, with windows at regular intervals. Through the windows, Pete could see skyscrapers. There was an entire city full of buildings, people, and even some flying cars!

It had been a while since Pete and Tito had tried to take herbal supplements in the Sandia Man Cave, but they'd certainly built up the place since he'd last come by. The crazy part was that they'd somehow done it without letting the people of Albuquerque know. Pete would have figured someone else would have driven out past Placitas at some point, but it turns out that no one had, or else he would have heard about this place. He was amazed.

Pete was flabbergasted. He didn't even resist the two pudgy white security guards cuffing him and Clara. When they tried to cuff Unk, the caveman almost tore the arms off the security guards. Clara stepped in and soothed Unk. She convinced him to "do what the nice man with handcuffs asks."

"This place is pretty awesome," Pete said to Clara, as they were escorted through the hall of exhibits. There was display after display about how the ancient cavemen had lived, farmed the land, and engaged in medieval warfare. Pete didn't even know how all that stuff had happened. He'd always thought cavemen were running away from dinosaurs.

Pete was more knowledgeable about dinosaurs than cavemen. The most he knew about the cave people was a Farside cartoon where a T-rex stuck its head in a cave, and spit out the men because they were smelly or something. His friend Tito had even tried to lie to him about Brontosaurs not being real, so he'd had to punch him. Pete had a dinosaur picture book from when he was a kid. He'd always looked at it when his parents were screaming at each other. Tito didn't even know how to read. Brontosaurs not being real was like Pluto not being a planet. Who would ever think Pluto wasn't a planet?

When they made it to the street level, the sight was breathtaking. There were skyscrapers that were taller than the Sandia Mountains. They seemed to stretch out endlessly in either direction. There were flying passenger vehicles whipping through the buildings overhead. It was like a swarm of insects flying through the city. Drones were dropping off packages on intake platforms for all the buildings.

A police car dove from one of the aerial traffic lanes and landed in a parking spot marked "FOR OFFICIAL USE ONLY" on the street in front of the museum. That's when Pete noticed there weren't any ground vehicles. The street had been repurposed into parking spaces for VIPs and city officials, and the rest of the space was pedestrian pathways with "native" foliage planted in manicured rows. It was like someone had designed a garden out of the forest that used to be growing in the valley.

The flying police car was marked "Tiwa Police." Pete had to assume that it was the Tiwa tribe, which if he remembered correctly, was the people from the Sandia Pueblo. They had a casino on the northern edge of Albuquerque. Two fit Native American police officers came out of the car and collected the prisoners.

"Did the casino pay for all this?" Pete said and indicated the city around them. He didn't think the Sandia Casino brought in that much money, but then again, Mötley Crüe had played a show there once. They were pretty much unstoppable, as far as bands went, so maybe it *was* possible to make that much money.

The two officers looked at each other while they were shoving everyone into the back of the cruiser. "You mean like the Tribal Casinos they have in Europe?" one officer said.

"I took a vacation to Germany once, went to the Streuselland Casino; I saw Hawkwind play," the other added.

"I like Hawkwind," Pete said as they shoved him into the cruiser.

The first officer ignored Pete and said to his partner. "Hawkwind? That grandpa band in the tight leather pants? Tribal casinos are like elephant graveyards. Aging rock stars go there to die."

"Hey! I like that kind of music!" his partner said.

"Yeah, Hawkwind will rock you like a hurricane, like the hurricane that ended their career."

"Shut up! That's their best song!"

"Hawkwind didn't write that song—" Pete said, but it was too late. The officers shut the door, and the three time travelers sat glumly in the back seat.

7

"There's something different about this city," Pete said, while the police cruiser skimmed through the buildings touching the sky. Unk's face was plastered to the window. He grunted with excitement.

"You think?" Clara said. "I figured we had just traveled to Rio."

"No, this isn't like Rio at all. There's a Jesus guy in Rio. I saw it on the Olympics. Do you think they have chimichangas in Rio? New Mexico has the best chimichangas. Even the Circle K chimichangas are better in New Mexico." Pete would sometimes "overshare," as his court-mandated therapist had told him once. Pete wondered if this was one of those times. Pete had had to see a therapist after the police had caught him walking the street with no pants. The police didn't believe him, that he had run out of change at the laundromat, and was just going home to get some more.

"Do you ever listen to yourself talk?" Clara mused.

"No. But sometimes I think in sounds, like, I tried to change the oil myself the other day, on my truck. Then I heard my father yell, 'You're doing it all wrong!' then spilled it all over the pavement." Pete shrugged.

Clara rolled her eyes and said, "You hear voices? Oh, god, I should have known. You're an escaped mental patient."

Unk saw a giant flying truck roar past. He hooted and clapped with joy.

"Great," Clara said. "I'm stuck in an alternate timeline with a mental patient, and a Neanderthal with the intelligence of a three-year-old."

"I'm not a mental patient, and I don't hear voices! Sometimes you just remember what your father said, but it's like he's saying it. Wait a second, what is that you said, about alternate history?"

"Did you not notice the flying cars?"

"I just thought it was a hidden city. Like the lost city of Cibola."

"First off, that's the seven cities of Cibola. Coronado was looking for the cities of gold. Second off, do you honestly think they could hide this on tribal land?"

"Hey, my buddy Tito says there's all sorts of stuff we don't know about, like, if you're so smart, who built the pyramids?"

"The Egyptians—"

"Ah hah! That's what you might think, being that they are in Egypt and all, but how did they move all that stone?"

"Oh, I don't know, slaves, beasts of burden, pulleys—pulleys—you remembered the pulley?"

"That's right! There's no possible way they could move all that stone. So it had to be aliens! How else could people build things?"

"Focus, Pete, focus. Did you remember the pulley?"

"Oh, that old thing. I didn't think we'd need it, so I left it in the cave."

"Are you telling me that you left a piece of technology much more advanced than anything from the time period, back in the Stone Age?"

"It's not like they can do much with it, just get up and down the elevator is all. It's not as if they're going to win any wars with an elevator."

Clara couldn't take it anymore. She flipped out. "It's a pulley! It's one of the fundamental building tools of the ancient world. The Greek temples, all of the castles, and even weapons like catapults were built with the technology of pulleys. You left a piece of technology in the past before it was discovered, and look at the results!"

Clara ended the speech with a grand gesture to all the buildings around them. There were skyscrapers as far as the eye could see. It was way bigger than Albuquerque. It looked more like Coruscant from Star Wars. The entire planet was one giant city.

"Oh, oh!" Pete said. "Does that mean they don't have food carts anymore?"

Pete couldn't remember if he'd ever seen food trucks on Coruscant.

Pete was separated from Clara and Unk at the police station during intake. The police docked in a large bay, at the hundredth floor of a large building. They scanned, poked, and prodded him. The police took his picture, and then he was unceremoniously dumped into an interrogation room.

After what seemed like hours, the door opened, and a woman walked out. She had large eyes as if she were the star of an Anime. She wore a bright blue miniskirt and had matching blue hair in pigtails. She had a white sweater with a ridiculously cute creature that wasn't quite a dog depicted in the center. For a brief moment, time stopped. It was just Pete and the girl.

He had never seen anyone quite like her. She was like every fantasy he'd ever had, rolled into one person. When he'd first met Clara, he'd thought she was cute, but when she didn't express interest in him, he'd given up. Pete gave up easily with girls. One time in high school, he'd asked the cutest girl in school out on a date. It turned out, the guy with the chiseled jawline standing next to her was her boyfriend, and he punched Pete out. Pete never asked out a girl again.

This girl was different. He would ask her out. Pete was in love.

She bounded to the table and sat down in front of Pete.

"Kon'nichiwa, O-Genki desu ka?" She had the most beautiful lilt in her voice.

"Will you marry me?" Pete stammered.

She laughed a carefree and amazing laugh. "You are too kind! I see that English is your preferred language. I will make note of that in your psych profiles."

"Psych profiles? I can explain! The only reason I have them is because my dad sent me to the pray-the-gay-away camp for a summer. He was worried when I didn't bring home girls, that I might be gay, but it was because I was embarrassed by my weight!"

"You look fine just the way you are."

"I do?"

"That's right! You're super fantastic!"

"How'd I get lucky to find a girl like you?"

"I'm a robot chosen by scans from your subconscious to make your police experience a more enjoyable one. I'm an MISAKO345B-C3-4714A-Q3."

"So wait, you're here to arrest me?" Pete said and shrugged. "I can think of worse ways to be arrested."

"Yes, there are plenty of worse ways. We seek to minimize negative perceptions of police work, by providing robots based on individual preference. In addition to being your arresting officer, I am also programmed as your lawyer, therapist, rehabilitation coordinator, expert witness, and PR manager."

"Why do I need a PR manager?"

"I will explain this to you because the lack of records indicates that you are not from around here, and may be unfamiliar with our customs. Since all high-profile cases are tried by a jury of their peers, in the form a national television voting-based reality show, each defendant has the right to a PR manager, and if they can't afford one, a PR manager will be provided by the court, criminal code-01-200-2245."

"Wait," Pete said. "You mean my trial is in the form of a reality show?"

"Yes," she said. "Research shows that reality-TV-based criminal justice increases positive perceptions of police work."

"But—"

"No time! We're on the air! Welcome to the Interrogation Room," she said in an ultra-peppy announcer voice. "We are going to have a trial for you tonight! We have an international terrorist, whose infamy knows no bounds. Not only did he try to destroy a national landmark, but he was also going after kids!"

"But I didn't do anything! I was just hanging out in the museum exhibit!"

"As your lawyer, I advise you not to say anything further," she said in a calm lawyerly voice.

"As you know, members of the public are encouraged to call in," she said in the announcer's voice. "It looks as if we have one on the line already. Hi, you're on the air."

"Hi," a voice echoed in the room. "I'm wondering, why is it always white people who commit terrorist acts? Is it their religion or something?"

"I'm only half white," Pete said. "My dad would always motivate me by asking me if I were a Mexi-CAN or a Mexi-CAN'T."

"Objection," her lawyer voice said. "My client's race is not on trial here."

She lowered her voice. It got thick and mean. She jumped up on the table and gave Pete a fearsome grin. "I'll tell you what's on trial—he sullied a national monument! Witnesses saw him, and his friends set off that bomb!"

"Whoa! Whoa! That wasn't a bomb!" Pete yelled.

"You think you can pull one over on me? Punk!" She switched again to a softer voice. "My client does not have to take that kind of bullying. You don't have to answer any of her questions."

She switched again to the tough voice and slammed her hand on the table. "Oh, yeah, I've seen a lot of dirt bags like you in my time!

You think because you've got a fancy lawyer, you're going to get away with it?"

"Whoa! Whoa!" Pete said. "I'm pretty sure this isn't how police questioning is supposed to go."

She responded with a smarmy voice, "As your PR manager, baby, I think you should go with it. Ratings say that people root for the little guy caught up in the big bad system. What's a little police brutality, if it means your exoneration?"

"But I seriously wasn't trying to blow up anything!"

"That's not the story the museum camera tells," the tough voice said.

A video appeared on the wall behind Pete. It was a camera view of the interior of the cave. It showed a flash, with the time machine exploding out of the portal, followed by Clara, Unk, and then Pete. There was an "ooooh" from an audience over the speaker.

The robot woman stood up and addressed the false mirror in the back of the room in her announcer's voice, "Is Pete guilty of domestic terrorism in a plot to destroy one of the nation's beloved landmarks? Find out, after a word from these sponsors."

The robot sat down, and said in a very reasonable, laid back voice, "—and we are off the air."

She lit up a cigarette and puffed the smoke. She didn't even look at Pete.

"What the hell was that?" Pete said.

"I'm on break. You can talk to your lawyer when we go back on the air."

"Right," Pete said. "So I guess I'll just sit here, then."

They sat quietly for a moment. Then Pete asked, "Have you got one of those?"

Pete usually detested tobacco products. One time he'd smoked pipe tobacco from a bong, because of a sticker on the side that said: "For Tobacco Use Only." Pete had turned white as a sheet, thrown up, and then passed out. He was pretty sure bongs weren't meant for tobacco use. Either way, it had left a pretty sour taste for cigarettes in his mouth. He hated it and vowed never to smoke anything tobacco-related.

However, since he was being put on trial, he figured he could make an exception. She pulled one from her pack and tossed it to Pete. She leaned over and lit his cigarette. After a few puffs and a bit of coughing, he put it out, and said, "I don't see how you can stand those things. Hey, aren't you a robot? Do robots even smoke?"

"What kind of question is that? Of course, we do," the robot said. Her voice was pretty sexy when she wasn't acting crazy.

"OK, so why do you smoke? They aren't good for you, you know."

"Burgers and fries aren't good for you either, but you don't see people giving that up. They just pump themselves full of anti-cholesterol and blood pressure medication."

"Eating is different from smoking! You can go without smoking, but not without eating. Speaking of which, do you have any food? I sort of skipped breakfast this morning. It's been a busy morning."

"I do make the best scrambled eggs."

"Everyone says that—" Pete said. If there was one thing Pete knew, it was eggs. He cooked them for breakfast burritos every day. There wasn't a better way to make them. Pete knew because he'd tried once. He'd used dehydrated eggs. They'd tasted like foam. Since then, he stuck to what he knew.

"I'm not everyone. I know I'm better at it than everyone else."

She'd started to grate on his nerves. Pete didn't like her attitude. She was attractive, but also seemed to think too highly of herself. Since there would be no possible way for her to make the eggs, Pete figured he'd challenge her, to shut her up. "Prove it."

She stood up and addressed the mirror and went back to the overly cheerful anime voice, "Welcome back! During the break, Pete tried to attack his arresting officer!"

"I did nothing of the sort!" Pete said.

She went into lawyer mode, "As your attorney, I suggest that you don't answer any intimidation tactics."

She jumped back into the cop persona, "I will end you, pretty boy!"

She then went back into the peppy announcer voice, "Whoa, whoa! Hang on there! We all know how conflict is handled in the Interrogation Room."

The disembodied voice of the studio audience yelled, "COOK-OFF!"

"That's right, a cook-off! The defendant will have a cook-off with the MISAKO345B-C3-4714A-Q3!"

- 37 -

The walls of the interrogation room lifted into the ceiling. They were surrounded by a live studio audience, on the set of a brightly colored cooking show. The backdrop was a swirling orange and red color. There were two ranges at the center of the stage. Native Americans, with a few people here and there of other races, comprised the studio audience. They were clapping and cheering wildly. The whole thing reminded Pete of a reality show he'd seen once where Americans had to compete on a Japanese game show.

After the cheering had died down, she explained the rules of the game to the audience. Pete would have to cook scrambled eggs. She would also cook the same thing, and a guest celebrity judge would decide the winner. When Pete asked about the prize he would get for winning, she smiled, and said in the PR voice, "Life not in prison, if they vote in your favor. It's all for your image, baby!"

The announcer's voice added. "Remember, vote for your verdict by texting 'guilty,' or 'not guilty' to 225115. Results will be tallied by the end of the program."

Once they were all situated in front of their range tops, the buzzer sounded, and they were off. Pete thought he had this in the bag. He had been cooking eggs every day of his life since he'd gone into business for himself. There was no way he could lose it, so he did what he did best: scrambled eggs with a pinch of salt, and the secret ingredient, a bit of cheese.

Once the buzzer went off, they lifted their hands up in the air. Pete finally took the time to check out his competitor's creation. The bot's looked different. It was moist, fluffy, and the steam wafted from the plate. By comparison, his was a hard clump of egg-stuff. Pete was nervous, but that didn't mean he was out for the count. When it came down to it, food was about the taste, and people liked his breakfast burritos; at least his mom did. They were going to like them even better, once they had Unk's seasoning.

The bot walked around to the front, then spoke with a French accent, "Bonjour, bonjour. I am the celebrity guest judge, head chef of the Lumières de Paris restaurant, and I will be judging these eggs."

"Hey, you can't do that! Isn't that a conflict of interest? I may be a terrorist, but I'm not stupid," Pete said.

"As your lawyer," she said in the soft voice, "I need you to refrain from incriminating language."

"I will end you, pretty boy!" she snarled in the cop voice.

She went to her egg plate first and smelled the eggs. She sighed and smiled. She took a fork and put the eggs in her mouth. Her eyes lit up, and she said in the French accent. "These are the best eggs I have ever eaten. Marvelous!"

She walked over to Pete's next. She shoved the fork into his and took a bite. She gagged and spat it out. "Oh yuck. Awful—simply the worse thing I have ever eaten."

Pete was offended. People could talk crap about the meat in his burritos all they wanted. They could spread rumors about grinding up rat, or failed freshman, all they wanted, but he drew the line at his eggs. There wasn't any way he could screw up eggs. He'd put cheese in them! "I demand a new judge! The system is rigged!" he cried.

He stormed over to her eggs. He would taste how awful they were. She'd probably forgotten the salt or undercooked them, or something. He put the forkful to his mouth.

"This is the worst cooking show that I ever—" He sputtered off, as the flavor of egg orgasmed in his mouth. It was amazing, like heaven come down in a cloud of egg, with the right amount of creaminess, and perfect texture. It melted in his mouth and was bursting with flavor.

Pete tossed his eggs on the ground, "They weren't that good, anyway."

The audience howled with approval.

She got the smarmy PR smile, "Brilliant, baby! They love you!"

Then she jumped into announcer mode and guided Pete back to the table. "Whoa! Did you see that? You never know what's going to happen in the Interrogation Room. We'll be right back."

The walls lowered from the ceiling, and the studio audience disappeared. They were back in the stark surroundings of the interrogation room. She lit up another cigarette.

"Where did you learn to cook like that?" Pete asked. He was captivated by her again. Pete had never thought he could go from loving to hating, to loving someone again so much.

"I guess it's a family thing. My grandmother made eggs for us. My father made them too. 'Just like grandma used to make,' he'd say, so I do too, I suppose."

"You have parents?" Pete said, amazed. He'd thought robots were like Terminators, rows of Arnold Schwarzeneggers, all coming off some factory line somewhere.

"What, and you don't? You just winked into existence one day?"

"Yeah, he kind of did—a few hours ago to be precise," a voice said from the corner of the room. The door was open, and a handsome Native American man stood in the entryway. He wore a suit and had short, no-nonsense hair. "Robot, deactivate."

"My client has a legal right—." The robot's eyes went dim, and she slumped in the chair.

"Hey," Pete said. "I was talking to her!"

"Your trial has been suspended indefinitely." The man had a long swift stride, and he was on top of Pete before he knew it.

"But I have the right to an attorney!" Pete said. He wanted to get the cute robot back. This guy was not as fun.

"People of the Great Nation have the right to an attorney, but since you don't exist, according to our records, I don't think we're violating anyone's rights."

"I do too exist! I'm from Albuquerque. My ID is in my wallet."

"That's exactly it. We looked at your ID cards. From the mountain range imprinted in the background, they look local, except that Albuquerque doesn't exist. Furthermore, you said you were Mexican. I'm afraid that's an ethnicity that doesn't exist either."

Pete thought back to something Clara had said. It was about pulleys or something. Since he normally wasn't a thinking man, it was a little bit hard for him. He knew there was something different about this world. It was something more than just a hidden city north of Placitas. That's when it hit him. He was in an alternate timeline! Just like when Biff had brought back the sports almanac and changed history in *Back to the Future II*. If Clara had led with that, he would have gotten it right away. Pete didn't understand why scientists didn't use movies to explain everything, instead of science.

Unfortunately, the man across from him came to a different conclusion. "From the absurd story, along with the strange behavior you've displayed since you've been here, we reached the conclusion that you're not human at all, but rather, a rogue robot—and we all know what happens to rogue robots."

The man jumped up and addressed the mirror. He put on a broad smile, and said with the support of the studio audience, "It's now time to play SMELT THAT ROBOT!"

- 40 -

The walls of the interrogation room rose again, and instead of a cooking show, there was a giant cauldron in the center, filled with molten liquid. Pete gulped. "Crap—um—do robots get lawyers?"

"No," the man said.

"Smoke breaks?"

"When we're done smelting you."

"Crap."

8

Clara could not believe that Pete had forgotten the pulley! She had made it abundantly clear that they could leave no traces of themselves in the past. Not only had she reminded him on several occasions but had spent many nights drawing on the cave floor the consequences of his actions. After he'd found sticky notes in the office clutter, she had used them to remind him what to take back to the future. He'd even made up a heavy metal song about what was written on the sticky notes. There was supposed to be no trace.

It was no wonder that heterosexual women complained about men's inability to do chores. Clara was glad that she had a genetic predisposition for liking women. She had trouble dealing with Pete during a simple time travel expedition. She couldn't imagine what it would like to be in a relationship with the guy.

So when Clara found herself across the interrogation room table with a middle-aged mum-bot, the robot sympathized with all of Clara's gripes about men. When Clara displayed her frustration about Pete's inability to follow simple, clear directions, the mum-bot wailed in sympathy. Her reality-TV-based trial eventually turned into a daytime talk show, where several middle-aged mum-bot women commiserated about their inability to have their husbands do anything useful.

Clara's ratings shot through the roof, and not only was she declared innocent to the terrorism charges, but she was offered a daytime television show and corresponding book club. She was about to interview a man who had been estranged from his family due to drugs, and finally came clean for the sake of his eight-year-old, when she realized that the entire premise of her having a show was stupid to begin with.

What Clara wanted to do was be reunited with her companions, figure out how she could travel back to the past, fix her timeline, and get back to Albuquerque before anyone knew she was missing. However, when she expressed her desire to quit the TV show, they stripped her of her wireless mic, and booted her from the interrogation room, with no direction where to go to find her buddies.

She stood in the hallway of a police station, in who-knows-what city, no closer to finding her friends, when she heard a laugh coming from down the hall. It was an unmistakable laugh. It was a deep, snorting laugh, which sounded more like a wild animal than a laugh.

However, she had heard that laugh many times. It was Unk's laugh, and he only did it when someone stumbled across one of his pranks.

Clara darted down the hall towards the laugh. Unk's attempt to prank a police officer could get him into serious trouble. Since justice in this version of the world all seemed to be based on popular opinion, she was certain that she could get Unk off the terrorism charges by claiming he had a disability, or something heartbreaking. However, if he began pranking police officers, there wasn't any way she could save face from that.

Even though Pete had brought Unk through time against her wishes, he was for better or worse part of the group now. She couldn't leave Unk in the past because he'd had experiences that would no doubt be considered religious to people of his time. Even an iPhone, to Unk's people, would be the voice of God coming down from the heavens. Clara did not want an ancient culture of people learning their values from cat and K-Pop videos on YouTube. She couldn't take the chance that Unk would describe what he had seen to the people of his time. Both Unk and Pete were her charges, and she needed to get them back.

The worst part would be if this world found out Unk was a living, breathing Neanderthal. There's no telling what they would do. However, based on her current experience of the reality-TV-driven justice system, it would most likely involve an autopsy, with grainy footage, and an announcer alluding to a government conspiracy.

She dashed into a room full of police officers. It was a typical precinct. There were rows of desks. Some people were cuffed for questioning. However, most of the officers crowded around their captain's office. Unk was inside, with a big grin. The captain raised a mug on his desk to his lips. Unk snorted with anticipation.

The color drained from Clara's face. Clara had seen this trick many times before. One of Unk's favorite pranks was peeing inside Pete's beverages. Clara attempted to push her way through the police officers that were gathered around, but the crowd was too thick. The captain was lecturing the group about policy and had lifted the mug several times without sipping. She called out to him, but he couldn't hear her. If she could only get through the group in time—

He took a sip.

The captain spat out his coffee.

"Is that urine?" he said and erupted with laughter. "You knucklehead. Come here, you."

The captain play-wrestled with Unk. The whole team bellowed with laughter and patted Unk on the back. They said things like, "Oh, that Unk," and "You got him good."

Unk pretended as if he were going to pee in another cup, and the entire group roared with laughter. They blurted out things like, "Oh, that Unk!" and "Such a crazy guy."

Clara's face crinkled with a dumbfounded expression. One of the officers turned to Clara. "Too much! Where did you find this guy?"

Before Clara could answer, another wave of laughter rippled through the crowd as Unk's antics intensified as he peed in a potted plant near the captain's desk. The captain almost died from the spasms of glee rippling through his chest. The other officers howled with joy when Unk turned his stream to a bookshelf behind the captain's desk.

"Um—" Clara decided to go with it. "I was wondering if I could get a ride back to the museum for my friends and me."

Unk stood on the desk and showered the captain with a golden stream, and the officers could not contain their laughter.

"Any friend of Unk's is a friend of mine. Oh, I can't believe he just did that! Did you see that!"

"Your captain seems to have a good sense of humor," Clara said as the captain laughed uncontrollably, while Unk danced around on his desk, spraying urine on all the other officers.

"The captain's great," the officer said. "He doesn't mind getting a little wet for a good laugh. Last year, he sat in the dunk tank—"

"Yeah, but urine—" Clara said.

"Oh, we all know that robots can't pee. It's just TV magic."

"Right—um—Unk—This nice man has offered to give us a ride. We probably should go around nowish." Clara pulled Unk down from the Captain's desk. There were groans of dissatisfaction as she pulled Unk away. They gave him high fives and shoulder chucks as they scattered back to their workstations throughout the office.

Once the Captain's laughter subsided to a mild chuckle, he sniffed his shirt. Clara turned to the officer, and said, "OK, yeah. Could you give us a ride right now?"

"Sure—" the officer said. "Hey, so where do you want to send the scrap from your defective unit?"

"The defective unit?" Clara said.

"Yeah, the Pete model. They're smelting him right now down in 4."

"What! Whoa! You can't smelt him!"

"I'm afraid that's not up to me."

"How do I stop it from happening?"

"You can't. He just has to pass an intelligence test, to prove that he's not defective."

"You'd better take me to him."

"OK."

"Now."

"OK."

———

Clara, Unk, and the police officer dashed down the hallway. There were a series of doors marked "Interrogation Room" followed by the numbers one through six. The doors were far apart from each other, and they had to run to get to Number 4 where Pete was being held. There was a sign above the door that said "RECORDING" in bright red letters.

Clara was about to go through the door when the police officer said, "Hey, you can't do that! Interrupting a live television event is obstruction of justice!"

She ignored him and pushed through the door anyway.

"I'm going to have to report you to the captain! I don't care how funny your friend is—"

Clara stumbled into a sound stage where a live studio audience was cheering and hooting, while Pete hung by his feet from the ceiling over a boiling cauldron. Pete slipped a few notches towards his fiery death, and the audience screamed with approval. A handsome Native American man with a big smile stood in front of the audience and attempted to calm them down.

Unk's eyes lit up at all the stimulus in the room. He ran towards the audience.

"Hey, get back here!" Clara yelled, and attempted to stop him, but was unsuccessful. Unk sat down next to a large man with a "SMELT THAT ROBOT" t-shirt and a big dopey grin. Unk slapped the man on the back, and the man smiled and slapped him back. They both stood up together and cheered. The audience chanted, "SMELT! SMELT! SMELT!"

Clara shrugged and saw a ladder leading to a catwalk. The rope that bound Pete's feet was tied to a large gear, with many notches, on the catwalk. Clara was about to ascend when a female who looked more like an anime character than a person stopped her. The woman held a cigarette in one hand, and said, "That's not going to help your friend."

"Why?"

"As his lawyer, and soon to be yours, too, I have to advise you that what you plan to do is obstruction of justice. That could get you smelted too."

"You call that justice! It's a circus!"

Unk started the audience doing the wave. They were all going wild. There was a Jeopardy-like question board on one of the walls. It had a couple of red spaces and one column of green spaces. Most of them were blue. The category with the green spaces was labeled "Metallica: Then and Now."

The announcer finally hushed the audience, "So, Pete, you're a Metallica fan."

"Oh, yeah," Pete said. "I've loved them since before I knew what music was."

"Well, that's fantastic. Have you thought of a new category?"

"I'll take 'Cooking,' for two notches."

One of the blue spaces flipped over to a question, and the announcer read it out loud, "What is a cooking device that heats food by the circulation of hot air?"

"Um—" Pete said. "Jeez. I don't know. I only have experience with food truck stuff. Could the question be about food truck stuff?"

A timer began ticking down. A melody accompanying the timer played faster as it got closer to zero. The audience hooted and laughed. The announcer shrugged and said, "I'm sorry, the questions are preset."

"A convection oven! Convection oven! What kind of cook doesn't know about a convection oven!" Clara yelled.

"Giving him the answers is interfering with a police investigation," the lawyer bot said plainly.

"That's not a police investigation! It's screwed up, is what it is."

"You're telling me!" the robot said. "Every time they shut me down—Do you know how long it takes me to reboot my circuits? What's worse is that I lose everything in my RAM drive. Makes finding car keys a pain."

"Look, you're a lawyer—Is there anything I can do that won't result in all of us being smelted?"

Pete was not doing well. Each time he got a question wrong, a buzzer would buzz, a square would turn red, and he'd slide down a few notches. His advantage gained via the Metallica questions disappeared. Unk did another stadium wave in the audience. At least *he* was enjoying himself.

Pete picked another category. "I'll take 'Replicant Voigt-Kampff' for ten notches, please."

The announcer began, "You're in a desert walking along in the sand when all of the sudden you look down, and you see a tortoise. It's crawling toward you. You reach down. You flip the tortoise over on its back. The tortoise lies on its back, its belly baking in the hot sun, beating its legs trying to turn itself over, but it can't, not without your help. But you're not helping. Why is that?"

"What do you mean, I'm not helping?" Pete said.

"Ooh," the announcer said. "I'm sorry."

The buzzer sounded, and the square on the scoreboard turned red. Pete slipped down ten notches and came perilously close to a bubbling surface of the molten liquid. He yowled in fear. The audience screamed and cheered. Unk seemed to notice Pete for the first time and paused for a moment. He pointed at Pete and laughed. This was a pretty good prank, as far as Unk was concerned.

"Well—There's one thing you can do to save him—" the robot said.

"What?" Clara said, "Tell me."

"I can't. I'll be disbarred. I'll never be able to practice law again."

"Look," Clara said. "I promise that no one will know. We'll be gone before anyone could piece together what happened."

"'Gone'—What do you mean, 'gone?'"

"Let's just say that I have a way to get out of the reach of any authority on this planet."

"Like off the planet?"

"In a manner of speaking, yes."

"OK, I'll help on one condition."

"What?"

"Take me with you."

"What? I thought you were worried about being disbarred!"

"I hate practicing law. I was just saying that, so I wouldn't get smelted."

"You're a robot!"

"I'm an MISAKO345B-C3-4714A-Q3."

"I'll just call you 'Misako.'"

"You're giving me a name?"

"What? No one has given you a name before?"

"Why? Do you name your car or your sofa?"

"Well, I did name my Toyota 'Yaris, the Black Pearl.' YAR-is, get it?"

"I get it! Like a pirate!"

"We'll have to work on humor with you."

"Taco Tuesdays." Pete said, and the audience "oohed."

"I'm sorry, that's incorrect," the announcer said, and Pete was lowered to the point where his hair was singed by the molten liquid bubbling underneath.

"OK, fine. We'll take you with us! Tell me what to do!"

"Follow me."

Misako and Clara walked out from the wings of the studio, onto the stage. The audience murmured, and the announcer's brow furrowed.

"What's this?" the announcer said. "I thought I'd deactivated you."

"Automatic reboot timer," Misako said. "I had it installed for when rude people like you shut me down without my permission."

"That's illegal technology."

"SMELT THAT ROBOT! SMELT THAT ROBOT!" the audience chanted, and went wild.

"Looks as if we've got another contender!" the announcer yelled, and the audience screamed with delight. More ropes fell from the ceiling, and two hulking robots came from the opposite wing. Their feet shook the ground with each step. They advanced on Misako and Clara. Unk saw they were in trouble, and dashed from the audience to the stage. He charged the robots with a wild howl, and they swatted him away with ease.

"I hope this wasn't your plan," Clara said as she backed away.

"Trust me," Misako winked. Two more robots came from the other wing of the stage. The audience jeered and screamed. Just as they were about to overtake the group, Misako proclaimed, "I invoke civil code ST34-ALPHA-2G!"

The audience and the announcer went silent. The robots stopped. The bubbling of the cauldron popped and sloshed. The announcer looked at the audience, and back at Misako. Then, with a loud scream, the announcer yelled, "IT'S TIME FOR SUDDEN DEATH!"

The audience chanted, "SUDDEN DEATH! SUDDEN DEATH! SUDDEN DEATH!"

The robot enforcers charged through the room and grabbed Clara before she could break free. She yelled at her newfound companion, "Sudden Death? What the bloody hell is Sudden Death?"

"Each contestant has the right to a fair and expedient death under civil code ST34-ALPHA-2G," Misako yelled, while the bots tied a rope around her feet.

"How is that helpful?" Clara said while they tightened her bonds, as well as Unk's.

"Some people would rather get it over with, just die, without all the stress and anticipation that they're going to die. Stress has been linked to bad health outcomes, you know."

"Yeah, but, when you're dead, it doesn't matter that—never mind. Tell me why are we doing this again?"

"We get one question for the four of us. Answer it right, and we all go home, with a nice prize package, too. Answer it wrong, and splat, smelting for all of us."

"I'd rather have several chances than just one. I knew I shouldn't have trusted a lawyer." Clara said, as they hoisted her upside down, and cranked her towards the ceiling.

"Trust me; it's much better this way. Statistically speaking, the more questions you have to answer on a trivia show, the greater the chance you have of getting them wrong. It's how they avoid giving away the top prize."

"This is not a million dollars. It's our lives!"

"Be that as it may, you still would have had to compete individually. The chances of all four of us all winning the top prize in a row—That's never happened. At least this way, we all can put our minds together, to try and come up with the answer."

The robots hoisted the others over the cauldron. The heat blasted Clara's face, and she immediately began to sweat. Her phone dropped from her pocket into the molten liquid. It burned within seconds of contact. When she was finally in place next to Pete, he said, "Hey Clara, I sure appreciate you dying with me and all."

"I kind of have no choice," she said.

"That's nice," Pete said. He wasn't paying attention to her. "I wanted you to know you're a good friend and all, but I wanted to tell you I'm sort of interested in someone else. I know we've formed a friendship over the past few weeks—"

"I like women, Pete."

"Oh—oh—OH!" Pete said. "I just thought that swimsuit calendar that came from your office was because you liked water sports."

"No, Pete. I'm a lesbian."

"All this time?"

"Yes, Pete, I'm kind of born this way."

"So it wasn't water sports. Hey, if we get out of this, I've got some Playboys that I keep under my bed. Perhaps you'd like to trade because I'm getting kind of bored—"

"Get on with it! What do you want?"

"I'm sort of interested in Misako."

"She's a robot."

"A robot—that's hot!"

The announcer thankfully cut him off before the conversation could continue any further. The announcer calmed the audience down, and said, "All right. All right! We have an entire group that has elected to exercise their right to Sudden Death! So let's not waste any time— Let's see that category!"

The board with Pete's question was wiped, and replaced with blue squares. One square was highlighted, and the category appeared over the top, "Sports Across Cultures." The announcer continued to explain the rules of Sudden Death to the audience. Clara cursed. She had never been much into sports, at least at the trivia level. She could probably name famous players, and maybe even some basic reasons as to why they were famous, but it didn't matter anyway. There was a slim to no chance that *their* sports resembled anything from *her* version of the world.

Most sports were solidified in the post-colonial world, at least in America. Sports like cricket were invented before England brought it over to the colonies, but in this world, the Americas colonized the world. There was no telling if cricket would even exist if the English were the colonized ones. For that matter, baseball and American football had definite European influences, despite their American origin. Clara was about to give up when she thought about Pete's scoreboard. One of the categories where he did well was Metallica, which didn't make any sense.

Metallica was an American band formed in San Francisco. They came out of a time when aggressive, no-bullshit music was popular. While Clara didn't go for that type of music, she knew that there was no way Metallica could exist both in this world and in her world. A world where Native Americans were the elite and had the technological advantage would have different popular music. Even on the off-chance that there was a band called Metallica in this version of history, there was no way they could be similar enough for Pete to get any answer right.

"Pete—" Clara said.

"What?" Pete said.

"How did you get that Metallica category? Did you ask for it?"

"Um—I don't know—I did have Metallica stuck in my head all day today. CHUN-CHA-CHUNG—CHUN-CHA-CHUNG!"

"I know! I know!" Misako said and wiggled on her rope. "The Death and Dismemberment Trivia Standards clause 107C says that trivia questions cannot punish ignorance or reward education."

"I don't get it," Pete said.

"They can't ask hard questions of stupid people. So they scan everybody's brain, and create trivia within their skill level," Misako said.

"Wait," Clara said. "So you're saying that it uses your own thoughts to create the questions and the categories?"

"In a manner of speaking, yes," Misako said.

"That explains a lot. I was just thinking, if you took a football, like an American one, and brought it to England, would they try to kick it?" Pete mused.

"Sports Across Cultures," Clara said. "Pete, you're brilliant!"

"I am?"

"Quick! Everyone think of rock-paper-scissors."

"What?"

"Just do it!" Clara commanded. Everyone stared at the scoreboard. Misako and Clara concentrated. Pete made the rock-paper-scissors hand gestures with his fist. Unk copied Pete and chuckled. The question appeared on the screen.

The audience "oohed," and the announcer said, "For the grand prize of your life, an all-expenses-paid vacation, and a mystery bonus prize: Who beats the fox at rock-paper-scissors?"

The audience was silent while the group thought about the answer. After a few moments, Pete said, "I don't know. I guess we're going to die."

"I don't know. I guess we're going to die. Is that your final answer?" the announcer asked.

"NO!" Clara screamed. "OK, I know this one. The Japanese had a game called sansukumi-ken meaning a three-way deadlock with fists, and there were a couple of variations—"

Pete glanced at Misako and said, "You have any idea what she's talking about?"

"Hey, just because I look Japanese doesn't mean I know anything about it. I only have what's in my programming, which is more a translation matrix than a cultural understanding." Misako shrugged.

"So if Kitsune, the fox, beats Shōya, the village head, then Ryōshi, the hunter, must beat the fox! Ryōshi! Ryōshi beats fox!" Clara exclaimed.

"That's correct!" the announcer screamed, and the crowd went wild. Confetti fell from the ceiling, while the cauldron was wheeled away, and several women in bathing suits came out on stage to untie them. "Tell them what they've won!"

A booming voice filled the room over the roars and chaos. "Not only have they won their precious lives, which they can enjoy for years to come, but in addition to the all-expenses-paid trip to Tahiti, they've also won A NEW CAR!"

A sleek red hover vehicle lowered from the ceiling, being driven by one of the swimsuit models. It was a smooth design, with a door that opened like a hatch. The audience hollered with excitement. The model stepped out of the car, and began to show it off, while the booming voice continued, "The new luxury S-E-S by Skyway floats through the city in style. With Accu-sense controls, heated seats, and automated—"

Pete turned to Clara and said, "How did you know the answer to that question? I only know enough Japanese to order at Teriyaki

Chicken Bowl, and even then, sometimes I have to say, the one with the chicken in the red sauce."

"I like writing Wikipedia entries."

"Wait—what?"

"I'm serious. Sometimes for fun, I'll learn about a subject I don't know much about, and compile enough information to either flesh out the Wikipedia entry that's already there, or create a new one."

"Sometimes for fun, I like to find beer bottles left in the desert, like from a party or something, and break them over rocks."

"You like to break stuff too!" Misako said. "I've always wanted to take a bat to my boss's computer!"

"Great," Clara said. "Two of them."

The recording light turned from green to red. The announcer walked off the stage. The swimsuit models went back to their dressing rooms. The crowd began to wind down and leave the studio. A few janitorial bots with sweeping and cleaning appendages rolled out to clean up after the show. Clara stopped one of the models, and asked, "How do we get out of here?"

"You can collect your prize down in Contracts," the model said and walked off.

"I don't care about the prize. I just want to get out of here."

"I care about it. It'd be pretty cool to have a new car. I wouldn't have to walk from the food truck to the parking lot again," Pete mused.

"We're going back to our own time—" Clara said, but was cut off by a swarm of police officers that burst into the room. The captain of the precinct was among them. He was rubbing a towel over his wet hair as if he had just showered.

"That was real urine!" the Captain said.

Unk laughed and pointed at the captain. One of the officers laughed, and when he saw the sour expression on the Captain's face, he shut up.

"What did you think it would be?" Clara said.

"He's a robot. I figured it would be coolant, or lemonade, or something," the Captain said.

"Why would a robot piss lemonade?" Clara said.

The Captain was about to respond, when the officer who'd laughed earlier said, "I've got this one, sir. What if it were a robot that pissed lemonade in a restaurant, so whenever you needed a refill the robot could just come and piss in your—"

"Ew. Ew. No! No!" Clara yelled.

The officer smiled and nodded to his Captain. The Captain smacked his subordinate alongside the head, and said, "Regardless, I'm taking you in for assaulting an officer."

"The female robots could serve milk—" the subordinate said, and got another smack.

"We've avoided being smelted before," Pete said. "You just watch us. We'll defeat whatever challenge you have for us—"

"Pete," Clara said.

"What?" Pete said.

"I don't think they're here to take us through the justice system again," Clara said and motioned towards the crowd of police officers. The rabble was fierce to behold. They were all holding pipes, chains, and other forms of bludgeoning weapons. They resembled a street gang more than a police force.

"But that's illegal," Pete said.

"I can't be humiliated on television. This doesn't make it to television. Boys," the Captain said and nodded to his men. They all advanced on the group, readying their makeshift weapons.

"Can they do that?" Pete said.

"I don't think now's a good time for an ethical debate," Clara said, as she backed away. "Misako?"

"Yes?" Misako said.

"Can you drive a hovercar?"

"I'm versed in over three hundred driving styles and—"

The police officers roared and charged towards them. Clara and the rest of the group dashed towards the car. Pete was the first one to the door. He opened it for the others and waved them inside. He dove in just after Unk squeezed his way through. The police officers collided with the car as it rose from the stage. The officers screamed and banged on the side of the car. The car hovered over to a window leading to the outside of the building. Misako punched the throttle, and the car crashed through the window to the outside world.

9

While they were in a high-speed chase through the city, Pete mused, "Is it stealing, when we won the car in a contest?"

"We crashed the car through a police station window," Clara said.

"Yeah," Pete said. "but hear me out. Can you steal from yourself? Like, say I have a pen. Then I take it from myself."

Misako dodged police cruisers, wove through a couple of buildings, and barrel rolled through oncoming traffic.

"How would you take it from yourself?" Clara asked.

"Pretend I took it from one pocket and put it in another."

"That's not stealing! That's putting in one pocket and then putting it in the other!" Clara yelled.

Their car dove a few hundred stories, screaming towards the ground, and at the last minute, Misako spun the car, narrowly missing being flattened. Two police cruisers crashed in flames, and the others scattered, to avoid a pileup.

Pete said, "What if one pocket is my pocket, and the other is your pocket. So I'm stealing it for you."

"Why would I have a pocket in your pants? That's gross!"

"You could be renting it."

"There's no reason anyone would rent pocket space. Do you really want random people sticking their hands in your pocket?"

"I'm sure there are plenty of urban dwellers that would pay for more storage space."

"That's why they invented backpacks."

"But what if you only needed one extra pocket. It seems like a waste to buy a whole backpack."

Before Clara could dignify Pete with a response, Misako lost the last police cruiser and crashed the car into the museum lobby, that was dark for the night. They made their way back to the Neanderthal display. Pete figured it would be a simple matter for Clara to fix up the time machine, and they'd be home for breakfast. When they'd arrived at the cave, the time travel parts were a jumbled mess, from being dumped through a time vortex. However, they were undisturbed after the incident in the museum, because it was still an active police investigation.

"So you're going to put it back together, or what?" Pete said.

Clara surveyed the shambles of the machine, "It took me weeks using prehistoric technology. There's no way I can sort through all this in less than a week, even with the best tools available."

"I can fix it for you," Misako said and smiled.

"I appreciate the sentiment, but it would take even longer to explain the intricacies of —"

"time travel. Yes, it's a time travel device. I've seen plenty. I think it's just a matter of taking the time stream converter and interlacing it with the transmitter shift matrix—" Misako began sorting through the junk at a pace that made even Clara dizzy.

"You've already invented time travel?" Clara asked.

Misako talked as she worked, "Sort of—"

"What do you mean, 'sort of'?"

"Well, it's kind of been taken over by the reality television stations."

"What is your obsession with reality TV?"

"At first, time traveler was a noble profession, like everything else, but it all changed once they'd had a presidential election with a candidate who was better at television than at political office. The election became a circus, but voter turnout was at an all-time high. That's when they realized that to get more voters, you need to make reality TV out of the presidency. All the other branches of government started following. Soon the channel that no one ever watched, where lawmakers would filibuster, was competing for ratings, so they had to spice it up. If a senator wanted a law passed, they would have to complete an obstacle course. So when time travel came around, who would want to watch a boring old historian attempting to verify the 'fact from fiction' of history? So, now they have shows where they send people back to smell the smelliest armpits of history or see if they can drink medieval city water without getting sick. Don't forget the great wars of history obstacle course shows."

"What is wrong with your society?" Clara said.

"I like obstacle course shows," Pete said. "Especially when they have wacky contestants, like when a guy dresses like Superman, but he can't complete even the first round. It cracks me up."

Clara shook her head. Before she was able to comment about the dumbing down of society, there was a shriek from Unk. He came running from the front of the cave. He grunted and pointed from where he just came. Clara went to investigate and saw police officers searching the building.

Clara retreated, and whispered to Misako, "You'd better hurry. The police are already here."

Misako's arms blurred with speed and dexterity. She grabbed pieces from the floor and assembled the time travel device. The police could be heard just down the hall, when Misako pulled out a device that was no larger than a football, with a strap attached to it for convenient carrying.

"That's it?" Clara said, confused.

"Yes," Misako said. "I had to make some adjustments to make it portable. The old room-sized time travel devices were pretty clunky."

"I always wondered about room-sized computers," Pete said. "You know like the kind they used when we first went to the moon. Were they computers, or did someone live in there, doing all the calculations?"

There were shouts from the front of the cave, "Police! Drop your weapons, and prepare for some exciting prizes."

Pete shrugged and walked towards the mouth of the cave. Clara grabbed him by the shoulder. She said to Misako, "Take us back to the last time coordinates we came from. Pete needs to get us a certain piece of technology we left behind."

"—but they said prizes," Pete said.

The police yelled, "Do you want to Double Down? Double the prizes, double the fun, double the consequences?"

Before the conversation could go any further, a time vortex appeared from the device Misako was carrying. It swallowed the group in one go.

"Or we can do Lottery of Death; the jackpot is up to a billion!" the police added.

————

Grek studied the strange twine-and-stone device. There were smooth, circular stones, threaded with twine. The strands attached to planks of wood that were smooth and rectangular. The stones were like no stones that Grek had ever seen. Even the river didn't make them round. The twine was like no tree root, and wood does not grow in boards. It was a mystery, but Grek was determined to figure it out.

When Grek's hunting party first saw that the hermit of the hills had visitors, they were cautious, and only sent scouts. The tribe had banished Unk when he'd sullied the ceremonial offering basket. The kooky hermit thought it was funny to watch the tribe crinkle their noses during the solstice ritual. When the pranks got to be too much, and the fear of angry gods caused too much anxiety, they left him where his pranks would hurt no one again.

However, the gods were angry, because the scouts reported tales of demons with powers of light and darkness. The hairless creatures could levitate objects, haul great burdens over vast distances, and did not slay Unk when he peed in their water skins. The gods must be punishing the demons, and Unk was the devil overlooking their punishment.

The tribe had decided to gather all the finest warriors to dispatch the devil and his ilk, once and for all, when the God of Light and Wind swallowed the evil for them. Grek's tribesmen decided to celebrate their victory by seeing who could piss farthest from the mouth of the cave. They were hooting with laughter, and punching each other, while Grek stared at the device left behind by the demons.

Grek knew there was something more to it than sorcery. If he could only figure it out, perhaps he could harness the powers of the demons. Grek had often mused that if the tribe could build caves, they would not be at the mercy of the gods so much. When the herds moved to places with no caves, and the storms decided to rage, the tribe would be wiped out. If they decided to stay in a cave like the hermit's, they would be protected from the elements, but the herds would move on. They would starve. If they could only create an encampment to keep the herds from wandering, and erect caves, they could have the best of both worlds.

Grek had seen the demons move stone with this device, and if Unk could fart in the face of the man-demon, and live to laugh about it, then this device could also be tamed. If Grek could only figure out how it worked. Then the idea came to him. If he pulled on the twine, the planks would move up and down. He was almost sure of it. He looked at his tribesmen. They were still peeing off the ledge of the cliff. This time, they were aiming at passing birds and hollering with laughter when they heard a squawk after connecting with their target.

Grek's hand trembled, as he reached towards the interwoven tree roots. He shook with anticipation. If he were right, this would be the biggest discovery in all of human history. Tribes everywhere would flock to his—village—No, 'village' was not the right word. 'City,'—he would call it a 'city,' and all the tribes would live together in peace and harmony. He had almost touched the twine when the male demon walked up from the interior of the cave.

"Hey, buddy," the demon said and began to pack up the device. Grek was too stunned by the reappearance of the demon to do anything but watch. The demon continued to chatter. "Clara wants me to get this. I'm worried that if I take it, Misako will disappear. I mean, I do need her for her egg recipe, but it's something more than just that. You know, it's like when you're watching anime, and you pop a huge boner, but then you think, 'That's a cartoon chick. I know she's not real. Why am I getting a boner?' Then you think that if she *were* real, you'd totally get a boner, but then you go, 'Wait a second; she's *not* real.' It's kind of like that, except she's a robot. Not that I have anything against robots. It's like she's real, but then she's not real—but then she is. Does that make any sense? Love's a strange mystery, my friend. Hey, buddy, it was a good chat. Don't let anyone tell you any different. I think you are an all right guy. You hang in there. It will work out for you. There's a girl out there for everyone—unless they're robots. But then again, robots are real. There I go again!"

The demon receded into the mouth of the cave holding the pile of strange material. Once the otherworldly creature's voice had faded into the blackness, Grek breathed a sigh of relief that the demon hadn't eviscerated him for daring to touch the demon's possessions. Just before Grek was able to recollect his thoughts enough to draw what he had seen on the cave wall, before he forgot about it, one of the other warriors dumped a poop bucket on Grek's head.

The others roared with laughter from the prank, as he spat out the waste, and picked it from his hair. He tussled with the prankster, and they all had a good laugh. By the end of the day, when Grek had some time to himself to think about it, the memory of the device was gone. He'd forgotten how it had worked, and the demons that could haul stone passed into legend.

10

A time portal appeared in the cave chamber. First, a pulley was spit out, and then lab equipment. Finally, a group of time travelers was dumped from the swirling vortex. Pete hit his head on the cave floor. Clara groaned. Misako sparked. Unk seemed to land on his feet though and laughed at the travelers who didn't fare so well. Clara untangled a length of rope that got stuck in her feet, and said, "You'd think if time travel were common in your time, they would have figured how to prevent us from being spit out like tennis balls from the time vortex."

"They could've fixed that problem, but slapstick humor gets good ratings with the audience. They can't wait to see how the travelers will fall on their faces each week," Misako said.

"Does everything in your society have to do with ratings?" Clara asked. She brushed herself off and walked towards the front of the cave. The rest of the group followed.

"How else would we plan our next war?"

"You decide who to invade on national television?"

"'Dictators in Paradise' is a big summer hit. Each dictator tries to find love while avoiding human rights violations."

"Is there anything you won't televise?"

"Spelling Bees."

"I sort of get it, but I mean, they televise Spelling Bees in my time period."

"Really? The Sharks get way more viewers."

"Like Shark Tank?"

"No, the vats they throw you into if you don't spell a word correctly. A booth of bees, a pool of sharks—"

"One time, Tito thought it would be pretty cool to own a shark, but then it bit his hand off," Pete interjected.

Both Clara and Misako stopped their conversation. Clara's head tilted in the "What are you talking about?" look that Pete had gotten used to by now. Clara shook her head and turned back towards Misako.

Pete shrugged and decided to tell Unk about all the cool places he could show him around Albuquerque.

"So, there's this giant cow. Some crazy rich dude just has a big statue of one in his front yard. It's called Whispering Pines Estate. I wonder if that's because the trees talk to him," he said as Clara held out her arm to stop him. "What?"

At the mouth of the cave, where there was normally a steel grate, rail, and a spiral staircase leading upward, was nothing at all. Pete would have gone over the edge if Clara hadn't been there to stop him. Sometimes, when Pete got to talking, especially if it was a topic that interested him, he lost all sense of himself and would run into objects.

However, there was nothing to slam into. From the absence of evidence of human occupation, the cave looked as it had in Unk's time period. However, the dirt road that went through the valley towards the cave was still there. The trail leading to the cave was still there. There were just no guardrails. They had stepped into a different reality again unless they had arrived before the guardrails were constructed for the cave.

"Misako," Clara said.

"Yes?" Misako said.

"You set the coordinates correctly? Back to the present?"

"Yes. Look; the device is configured correctly."

"Pete?"

"Huh?" Pete was roused from his thoughts. He'd been wondering if mice liked cheese, would they then like pizza?

"You got the pulley? Every single scrap of modern technology?"

"Yeah, I promise. I didn't leave anything behind. Well, except maybe my poop. We did poop in the woods while we were back there. You think that could have changed things? Maybe they would find my fossilized poop, and get my burrito recipe?"

"I don't think our poop is going to change anything—"

"Yeah, but what if they figure out my recipe before I'm alive to invent it?"

"First off, there are no scientists figuring out recipes from scat. Because, well, ew."

"You don't know that! There are some fast food places that taste like poop."

"All right; moving on. Misako, do you think there could be a faulty circuit, or something wrong with the device?"

"Sure," Misako said. "I did make it in a rush. I mean, everyone knows that child labor is well suited for making portal electronics. Their hands are small enough for working with tiny devices."

"Let me guess; you televise it."

"You put children on TV? That's sick!"

"Hey, maybe we should explore?" Pete said. "I mean, we *are* here, and perhaps we can learn something about this time period."

"You just want to make sure no one stole your burrito recipe," Clara said.

"That too."

"OK, fine. Take Unk and explore. If you see any humans at all, come right back here—"

"I will!"

"—and don't leave anything behind!"

"I promise!"

"—and don't interact! You observe only!"

"Will do!"

Pete paced back and forth at the cave entrance. After a few attempts to try and lower himself onto the sheer rock wall below, he turned back to Clara and Misako, who were pulling apart the device.

"Um, Clara," Pete said. "Can I set up the pulley again? I'm not good at rock climbing."

Clara rolled her eyes and nodded.

"Woohoo!" Pete said. "Come on, Unk. Help me get this together!"

11

Pete and Unk traversed through the valley in the Sandia Mountains. The air was cool and crisp; the leaves had already changed for the season. Flocks of birds, on a break from flying south for the winter, could be heard among the trees.

Unk fell back into his role of tracker and guide, as the region hadn't changed too much since his time. The mountains moved on geological timescales that made human life, even human empires, seem insignificant. Pete pondered his own insignificant place, in the autumn chill, when a primal shriek pulled him back to reality.

Up ahead was a parking lot. Pete knew the parking lot well. It was the last paved road before the dirt road that led up into the mountains. A tan Honda Civic pulled up to a spot in the empty lot. Unk cowered behind Pete in fear.

"It's OK," Pete said. "That's just a car. It looks as if we made it back to the right time period."

A man stepped out of the car. He looked more as if he were an extra in a Mad Max movie than a person going for a Sunday walk. He was wearing a leather jacket, had thick greasy hair, and a shotgun slung over his back. That's when Pete realized the parking lot was overgrown and cracked, not at all like the one they had left behind. The man saw them and pulled his gun.

"Stop right there!" the man said.

Pete held up his hands, and Unk did the same.

"We don't mean you any harm," Pete said.

"So why are you out here on my land?"

"This is a National Park."

"What are you talking about? The National Park laws were repealed years ago!"

"So that means it's OK to bring beer to them?"

The man walked closer and pressed his shotgun against Pete's head.

"Where did you get that hat?" the man inquired.

Pete moved to take "The Perfect Burrito" cap off his head, and the man pressed the weapon harder. Pete thrust his hands into the air.

"I had it custom made," Pete croaked.

"I don't like it when people lie to me."

"Seriously, I made it to remind me that anything is possible."

"That's the stupidest thing I ever heard."

"No, really, watch, put the hat on. That's right; you can still point the gun at me while you do." The man awkwardly put the hat on, and Pete continued. "So, it's a little trick I learned when I started my own business."

"You own your own business?" The man sounded intrigued.

"Yeah, I did it just by repeating these words every day. Just look up at the clouds and say, 'I am ready to go ahead now.' Anytime you're ready—Now would be a good time, Unk—to get ahead of a certain person distracted by my ploy, and knock him out. Anytime you're ready—"

After a moment of attempting to decipher what Pete was trying to say, Unk decided the best course of action would be to clunk Pete over the head. Unk's wild animal laughter was all he heard as he faded into unconsciousness.

––––––––

Clara and Misako decided the best course of action involved running diagnostics on the device. Misako sat cross-legged, surrounded by the pile of junk that used to be Clara's lab. Most of the parts were a jumbled mess, after being ejected from the portal for the fourth time. Clara was surprised that there was anything that could be salvaged at all, much less enough to make a functioning device.

"Well, I don't think there's much we can do with this," Clara said, picking up a circuit board that was smashed.

"Ooh!" Misako said and pulled the board away. A slot on Misako's arm opened, and there was a circuit board tool kit inside. "The data chip is still working on that board! I can give the device WiFi, maybe even a data connection!"

"You have a toolkit built into your arm?" Clara asked.

"Of course, how else would I make self-repairs?"

"You don't let anything get you down?"

"Nope; once I give the device data, I'll be able to make some scans, and do some diagnostic tests. Your original device was a genius design, very elegant compared to the first time travel device invented in my time."

"Thanks," Clara said, but she couldn't take all the credit. The original design of the machine had been partially her professor's, and partially her idea. When she had begun her underpaid-for-her-skill-level life of a graduate student, the machine was almost finished. It was

Clara that had connected the key dots together and saved a project that was going nowhere. However, like most graduate students, her professor would get all the accolades, and she'd be lucky if she'd get another semester of paid tuition.

The worst part was that even though her professor shouldn't have been hitting on a graduate student, and even though she had clearly outlined that she had no interest in men, as if blasting The Indigo Girls in the lab wasn't enough, she *still* had no one else that understood physics quite like him at school. In an effort not to shrivel up with loneliness, with no one else to talk to about the ideas floating in her head, she often would seek his company. When he wasn't a perv, he wasn't bad, and when he wasn't bad, she'd play The Beatles, a band they both liked. Maybe that had been her mistake, making any attempt to connect to the guy at all.

Clara and Misako worked well into the night. As they worked and talked, Clara became more and more interested in what Misako had to say. Not only did she understand physics at the level Clara understood it, but there seemed to be a lot of parts to her that Clara found intriguing. When they talked, it felt as though they had been talking for hours, and had known each other their entire lives.

At first, Clara was irritated with Misako, not because of her bubbly personality. It was quite endearing for someone of her intellectual equal to be refreshingly optimistic. Most of her peers were quick to find fault with the world, and throw up their hands at the impossibility of fixing it. Whereas Misako would roll up her sleeves and get to work, and Clara liked that in a woman.

The part that irritated Clara was not her personality, but rather the design of her exterior. Misako was hot but in a heterosexual-fantasy-woman type of way. It was as though Misako were designed to be the woman of every asianphile's dream. Clara would have picked up a woman like Misako in a nightclub in a heartbeat, but knowing that she was manufactured and that some skeazy, overweight, middle-aged anime nerd would be taking her home, irritated her.

Clara felt as though Misako were designed purely for the pleasure of others when there was so much more going on in such an incredible woman. Even though they were risking pollution of the timeline by taking her from her world, Clara was glad she had, more for the sake that Misako would be able to live beyond her programming and live the life that she wanted.

"Hey, Misako," Clara said

"Yes," Misako said and looked up from a stream of code she had been tweaking. So far every test indicated that they were in the right time period, and that there was nothing wrong with the device.

"You know you're free now," Clara said.

"That's why I came with you. I wanted to be more than just my programming."

"Yeah, but I mean—Pete's a good guy. I don't think he'd take advantage of you in any way. I just want you to know that you don't owe him anything. Even if you feel as though you do."

"Pete would charge for freeing me?"

"No, it's just that I can tell he likes you, and even you might be programmed a certain way."

"You mean like sex?"

Clara's face became very red, "Yeah, I just didn't—"

"You think I exchange favors for sex?"

"No, I just mean that you might have been programmed."

"What? Are you a robocist?"

"No, I just mean, the way you're dressed, and your eyes."

"Whoa! Whoa! So now you're judging me for how I dress!"

"No, I just mean that guys can be pigs."

"Well, I don't know how it is where you come from, but robots have rights, you know! Do women lawyers who dress nicely from your time just throw themselves at any old man?"

"Don't you lecture me about feminism!"

"I'll have you know that I prefer women."

"You do?" Clara said, a little taken aback. Not only had she misjudged Misako, and felt like an asshat for doing so, but she needed her gaydar checked. Clara always knew. She had never inadvertently hit on a straight woman, or misidentified a lesbian in her life. Of course she usually also only dated on Goodreads, where most people had social media identify their gender preferences. However, she must have had some preconceived notions about artificial intelligence, because she had just assumed men had designed Misako for men.

"Look," Misako said. "I can't choose how I'm made, much as you can't choose how you're born. All I can do is be the best I can be, given my operating parameters."

"I'm sorry. I've never met a robot before. I had just assumed the worst about your programmers, not about you."

"No, it's OK," Misako said. "I see what you think about robots. We're just machines—made up from parts—and to think—I was starting to like you!"

Misako walked over to the front of the cave, and Clara followed.

"Misako, wait!" Clara called out to her, but it was too late. Without looking back at Clara, Misako jumped from the edge of the cave, off the cliff. Clara ran to the edge and peered over, terrified of what she might see. Instead of a jumbled mess of robot parts, she saw Misako on the valley floor, running off in the direction Pete had gone, with tears streaming from her eyes. Misako disappeared into the night before Clara could even think about going after her.

12

Pete heard the erratic thump of an unkept road from the trunk of the car. His head ached from the wallop Unk had given him. The jostling of the car didn't help the pain much. He felt as though he were on a backcountry road leading to nowhere.

He could hear voices in the front of the car. They were distant and muffled. He heard the unmistakable laugh of Unk, followed by the voice of the man with the shotgun. "That's certainly the best taco I've ever tasted. Whatever spice you put on it, well, that just hit the spot. Hang on. Getting a call. Yes, sir. No, sir. I didn't see her. I got the man, and the caveman, as well as the spice."

The man was stealing Pete's spice and his caveman! Pete needed to get out of the trunk. Even though his hands were tied, the man hadn't bothered to bind Pete's legs, so he was able to kick at the trunk. The man was too busy talking to Unk to hear the thumping coming from the back.

"I think this hat is lucky. Maybe the perfect burrito is within reach," the man said.

The bastard was stealing his hat! Pete cried out, kicked with a powerful thrust, and the trunk burst open. He jumped from the car and rolled out of the way of a pair of headlights. A few cars sped past him, honking. Pete stood up in the center of the road and realized that he wasn't on a back road after all. He was on I-25, heading south into the heart of Albuquerque. Cars swerved around him, and one person even yelled, "Get out of the road!"

However, Pete was too stunned by what he saw to do anything but gawk in the middle of the interstate. The Albuquerque he had known for his whole life, that was displayed in exterior time-lapse shots on shows like Breaking Bad, was no longer. It now looked as if it were out of a dystopian novel.

The roads were cracked and in a state of disrepair. Half of the buildings were ramshackle as if they belonged in the post-apocalypse. Others were garish and grand, as though they were trying to invoke the splendor of the Roman Empire, along with the wealth of Dubai. One theme seemed to link all the buildings together: it was burritos.

There were advertisements on every billboard, and signs on every building: "The Professor's Breakfast Burritos: Taste Perfection." On all the billboards was a picture of 'The Professor' himself. It was the man who had died in Pete's arms, the professor who had invented time travel. Not only was he alive, but he had stolen Pete's idea.

Before Pete could walk in a daze to the nearest Professor's Burrito Shack, and into the oncoming traffic that had been avoiding him up until this point, a hand grabbed him by the shoulder and yanked him over to the edge of the highway. Misako pushed him over the highway wall, and they tumbled onto an overgrown frontage road, with an abandoned strip mall.

Misako belted out in her tough cop voice, "What the hell are you doing! You could have gotten yourself killed!"

"I might as well be dead," Pete yelled.

Misako switched to her more sympathetic voice. "Don't say that. Why are you saying that?"

Pete motioned to a fast food joint up the highway. It was a temple worshiping the might of the burrito and the power of fast food. There were giant golden columns towering over the entrance, illuminating the night sky. It was a burrito oasis to hungry travelers and dinner-seeking families. "That's why I'm saying it."

"A Burrito Shack?"

"Not just a burrito shack! *My* Burrito Shack! It was my idea to make the perfect burrito, but the professor stole that from me!"

"You're saying the timeline isn't correct?"

"Yeah, for one, the professor is dead. He died the night that we first time traveled."

"You mean like that guy?" Misako said, and pointed to a billboard of 'The Professor,' looking as dignified as a Colonel Sanders wannabe could look, holding a burrito.

"Yeah," Pete said. "He was the guy that originally invented time travel."

"You mean Clara didn't invent it?"

"She helped. Well, as much as she could help, considering her pervy professor and all."

"Wait? What?" Misako said. "So you're saying she had a male figure of authority abusing his privilege to make advances on her?"

"Yeah, that's how she tells it."

"That's wonderful!" Misako said, excited.

"That's wonderful?" Pete said.

"I just thought all this time that Clara was a stuck up jerkface who was jealous of me because I knew more about time travel than she did. However, it turns out that she's just projecting her past experiences on me!"

"So, how is that wonderful?"

"It means there's a chance for us to make it!"

"Wait, so you like her?"

"Like her? I LOVE HER! I WANT TO SING ABOUT HER TO THE HEAVENS. LOVE LIFTS US UP WHERE WE BELONG. LIKE EAGLES CRY. ON THE MOUNTAIN SIDE."

"Why eagles? Don't they kill other animals?"

"Come—we must buy her a ring—will you be the best man at our wedding? Is gay marriage legal in your time?"

"Whoa! Whoa! How do you know she's the one? You've only known her for about three hours."

"Well, that's easy; my brain is a vast quantum computer artificial intelligence able to crunch large datasets to make better decisions. In the space of this conversation, I've run simulated scenarios of our married life five hundred thousand times, with only a 10.03% divorce rate, 2.3% chance of infidelity, and a 0.01% chance where one or both of us end up dead from uxoricide."

"But doesn't love just happen, like eagles on a mountain or something?"

"I inputted variables including two partners meeting through a mutual misunderstanding, our education, experience level, and the plot of every Meg Ryan romantic comedy."

"You have Meg Ryan in your timeline?"

"No, just after Clara and I had a fight, I subscribed to this service called Netflix, and watched every romantic comedy simultaneously while crying into a bucket of what you call Fro Yo."

"Right—so um—I have experience with this—I saw this one movie with Ben Affleck and JLo, and through the power of his masculinity, he totally convinces JLo to sleep with him. I tried that once at a gay bar, and all these dudes hit on me—none of the women. It totally didn't go the way I thought it would. So movies aren't like real life."

"However, she's *got* to love me. I'm perfect for her! There's a 99.9% accuracy in my marriage analysis."

"Yeah, but being perfect for someone doesn't mean they like you. There was this one chick Betty, who I met at the emergency room. She threw out her neck headbanging at the same Metallica concert I was at. Two metal heads with the same neck injury from the same concert? How could it not be love? So I went for it, and kissed her right then and there."

"Let me guess. She had a girlfriend."

"No. No! I don't always hit on lesbians. I've just been unlucky with you two. It's cool, by the way; I know I liked you, but I won't let it get awkward. I just don't have gaydar, is all."

"Remind me to build you one. So what happened with the woman?"

"She had a giant boyfriend named Tor, and a bottle of mace in her pocket, but the point is that you can't control who falls in love with you, and if you come on too strong, you're bound to scare her off."

"So you're saying that if I propose to her, I might get maced? You humans have a weird way of expressing your emotions. Robot dating is so much simpler. We usually find compatible partners after the first hello."

"Well, humans can't process all that fancy quantum whatever it is. So you have to move slowly with us."

"Thank you for the dating advice! Come! We must get back to Clara."

"What about Unk? He was kidnapped by some crazy biker guy in a Honda Civic, or was that willingly went with him? It's hard to tell with Unk."

"Clara first. Unk can take care of himself."

Misako dragged Pete by the hand. They walked North on I-25 back towards where the road splits off towards the Sandia Man Cave. Pete sighed. Misako was the second woman that he had briefly fallen in love with that turned out to not like men at all. Pete wouldn't let it get to him. He'd been rejected by so many women. It was hard to count them all. Maybe he would take her up on the offer of getting gaydar. Or maybe he'd just settle for a -dar that would point to women who weren't totally opposed to the idea of dating Pete. The perfect woman had turned out to be like the perfect burrito, elusive, and just out of reach.

Unk wasn't sure what to make of his new companion. As an expert practical joker, Unk was pretty sure that there was a hilarious prank forthcoming. Why else would the man with the metal stick want Unk to knock out Pete? When they threw Pete into the bowels of the metal beast, Unk was pretty sure that he'd gotten the joke. Pete would wake up in a pile of poop, and the expression on his face alone would be worth it.

However, when the man convinced Unk to ride in the beast, he realized the joke must have been on him. The metal stick the man carried wasn't a stick at all, but an explosive device that could shred trees. Unk thought perhaps it was a cruel joke. He expected Pete to crawl out of what the man called a trunk, and they would all have a laugh. However, as the beast kept "driving," and Pete was no closer to emerging, Unk became afraid. He tried to appease the man, by using some of the spice that Pete liked so much on something called "tacos" that they bought at a "drive-thru." The flavor seemed to get the man more excited.

Unk remembered people like this man from his past. The men of his village were like him. They were too serious all the time, and couldn't take a joke. When Unk had swapped the dead ceremonial herd beast for a small flightless bird, before the winter sacrifice, the villagers had thought that he had angered the gods. Unk had thought, how could they be gods, if they didn't have a sense of humor?

The villagers didn't take too kindly to his jokes. They had dragged him from town and left him tied to a stump for dead, as a sacrifice to appease the gods. However, Unk could pop his thumb to escape any ropes, and he wasn't lost to the blazing sun of the desert. Instead, he had wandered to the foothills of the great Mountain and found a cave. He was living happily on his own until the travelers came.

One was a woman of mating age, and the other was his new best friend, Pete. Unlike his village, Pete seemed to enjoy his shenanigans. He even didn't try to compete with him for the mate. However, once a new female had joined the crew, Unk had realized that the one he'd thought would be his future mate liked other females. It wasn't that big a deal. Mates come and go; best friends are forever.

Unk was well on the way to hatching a plan to escape with Pete back to the females when the man pulled up to a strange cave. It wasn't like the home in the cliff, but rather a cave that seemed to be sized to the metal beast. It opened a maw, and let the beast through. Unk was scared at first, but he needed to be strong, for Pete.

Once they were out of the beast, and inside what the man called his "garage," they opened the "trunk" to look for Pete, and he wasn't there. The man was upset at first, and began waving the metal stick around, but calmed down when two tiny humans wandered into the garage to meet the man. They hugged him, and called him "Daddy."

Unk would have thwacked them, and made his escape, except that the man asked Unk if he'd like some turkey. Now *that* was a word that Unk could understand. From the smell inside the cave, the hunt of the man's tribe seemed to be fruitful, and there was a turkey roasting in a fire pit they called the oven.

Unk figured he could thwack the man and his tiny humans later. He was hungry and wanted to eat something. The man beckoned Unk inside, and that's how a typical suburban family invited a caveman to dinner.

———

Clara stumbled through the woods in the dark. The walls of the canyon prevented even the moonlight from poking into the forest floor, so she had to use the dull glow of the time travel device's input screen to guide her through the valley. Luckily, there were only two directions she could go, further into the mountains, or down towards the desert. She was heading out of the mountains, towards the tumbleweeds and cacti. Once out, the moonlight would light the way.

She scraped herself on more than one occasion, by bumping into a branch she'd missed, or stumbling on a log in the game trail. It was better than waiting in the cave for one of her companions to come back, which in the dark was scarier than woods. The trees at night seemed ominous, as though they were reaching for her.

As a scientist, she attempted to put her fears away, by reminding herself that they were artifacts of a primal brain, that was designed for hunting and gathering. In practice, she felt a pit in her stomach and chill come over her, every time she saw a gnarled branch or a spooky shadow.

It was slow going, and dangerous, considering she didn't know what kind of medical treatment was available in the time period in which they'd appeared. Clara wasn't ready to believe that they were at the correct date.

They'd taken all possible precautions to preserve history, and left nothing behind—unless Unk was the change. Was he destined to sire children? From his living situation as a hermit, Clara doubted it. From the looks of it, Unk was in his early twenties, which would be an old man by prehistoric standards. Living into their thirties was about as much as anyone could ask for, and if he did have kids, he would have already had them. Most ancient people had had children the moment they were reproductively capable.

The other explanation for a possible change was the butterfly effect popularized by Ray Bradbury, where even small changes, like stepping on a butterfly, could have large impacts on the timeline. Clara and Pete both ate animals, killed bugs, and left their human waste behind. If the butterfly effect turned out to be real, then they would never get back to their timeline, because their very existence in the past would change things.

However, for the sake of her sanity, she had to believe that a dead bug in the past wouldn't affect the timeline in any noticeable way. She had to believe that so long as she didn't change the course of human history, time would be unchanged by people traveling through it, just as campers in a national forest don't destroy the ecosystem of the forest by swatting single mosquitoes that happen to fly into their campsite.

She saw the canyon walls recede to either side as she neared the outer edge of the forest. She was no longer in the shadow of the cliff, so she was able to stuff the time travel device in her pocket, and navigate by the moonlight. She was about to come out of the tree cover when she heard a twig snap.

"Hello?" she said, ignoring all her survival training from her father. The last thing she wanted was to alert the local wildlife to her presence.

There was a rustle in the bushes, and the unmistakable sound of something moving.

"I have a gun," she lied, and whirled around, unable to pinpoint where the noise was coming from. She contemplated running but felt that would be a mistake in the darkness. She regretted not staying in the cave. However, Clara was never any good at waiting. She always wanted to be doing something. Even while she waited for a computer to crunch the numbers on the experiment, she would engross herself in another task, teasing out another theory. From sunup to sundown, Clara kept herself busy. Her need to keep busy would be her undoing. She should have waited until morning to leave the safety of the cave.

The movement shot towards her, and she whirled around, just in time to see a shadowy figure approaching. She didn't think and struck the figure with her fist. The assailant huffed, and she whirled around with a kick to the chest. The person stumbled backward. She kicked again with the ball of her heel and heard the crack of teeth echoing throughout the forest. The figure dropped to the forest floor and groaned.

She pulled out the time travel device and used the light of the screen to get a look at the person's face. He was wearing a puffy winter coat, hat, and gloves. She had to bend down to get a look at his face. It was the professor! He wasn't dead.

"Nice to see you, too, Clara." He smiled and spat blood from his mouth.

"Professor!" Clara said and helped him up to his feet. "How did you—? What—?"

"I figured you might end up here after the accident in the lab."

"But how—I thought you—"

"Had died? Hardly. Your traveling companion is hardly a medical professional."

"OK, so you lived, but why here? How would you think to come here of all places?"

"I had set the coordinates for the time of Sandia Man. I had always been fascinated by the cave, ever since my third grade class took a field trip there. I wanted to know what they were like, how they lived, whether they were ancestors of modern-day Native American tribes—I figured my first trip to the past better be in a time period where I had the least potential to have my presence alter history. So when I came to and saw the device had worked, I knew it was only a matter of time until you came back here. Hey, look, I'm sorry about what happened in the lab that night. I was out of line."

Clara almost couldn't believe her ears. Had she somehow stepped into an alternate timeline where the professor wasn't an asshole?

"Yeah—OK," Clara said. She didn't know whether he was sincere in his apology but was willing to give him the benefit of the doubt. The situation was difficult, as she had contributed to a major scientific discovery. Her name would be on the paper that heralded the breaking of the time barrier. Her career would be set, and she'd no longer have to put up with unwanted advances, but at the same time, she felt that she shouldn't have had to put up with his "affection" in the first place. She decided to play it out the same as any other time she'd spurned his moves, wait and see. He could apologize all he wanted, but his actions would speak louder than words.

"Let me drive you back to Albuquerque," the professor said. "There's something I want to show you."

"Sure," Clara said, and they began walking towards a parking lot. There was something troubling about the situation. It went beyond the question of his sincerity. History had changed. The cave lacked the safety railing that was there in her proper time period. If history had changed, and she was the cause of it, Clara couldn't figure out how the professor could know about events from her timeline.

She believed that in this new version of history, people hadn't discovered the cave. Unk *could* be the Sandia Man. If he hadn't died in the past, then there would be no remains in the future. If there were no Sandia Man, then how could the professor have gone there as a child?

There was no possible way *a* professor from this current version of history had gone to the cave as a kid. *This* professor was not from this timeline. As if to accentuate her thoughts, when she turned to ask him a question, she was met with a gun.

"I knew you'd figure it out before we got to the car," the professor said. "I should have led with the gun."

He waved the handgun at her and motioned for her to keep walking. Clara turned back towards the car. The forest turned into the high desert landscape of tumbleweeds, cacti, and low scrubby bushes. She needed to think of a plan. Misako, or at the very least, Pete, would be back in this direction. She had to leave a clue that she was in trouble. Better yet, she should let them know that it was the professor that they were after. She stuck her hand in her pocket.

The professor said, "Nah-ah-ah! Take your hand out of your pocket!"

Clara pulled the time travel device from her pocket, and began to fiddle with the coordinates, while saying, "I just thought that you might want this."

"So you can suck us back into the past, and get the drop on me? I don't think so. Toss it here." He held his palm out.

"Look, I set it for 1965," Clara said, and showed him the display, while she set the day and month. "That's well before any of this."

"You and I both know that the time portal isn't exactly a smooth ride, and you'd use it to get the jump on me. Now throw it here; then maybe I won't shoot you and come take it for myself."

Clara threw the time machine, but not towards the professor. She tossed it away into the bushes. She ran in the opposite direction, and her captor was faced with a choice. He could either run after her or go for the device. He decided to go after her and booked it towards her.

The events of the last couple of days had drained most of her strength. She didn't get very far before he got the drop on her. He tackled her; she crashed to the ground, narrowly avoiding a face full of cactus. He lifted her to her feet and jammed the gun into her back. He looked back and forth for the time machine. The landscape looked the same in all directions. If he wanted to find it, he'd have to look through every single bush.

"Stupid woman," he hissed. "I'll just come back in the daylight and find it. You've accomplished nothing."

Clara didn't say anything. He shoved a gun in her back and pushed her towards a car waiting in an overgrown parking lot up ahead. He was wrong about what she'd accomplished. Misako would be able to pinpoint the location of the device. From the way she'd run from Clara earlier, the android had excellent night vision and would be able to spot it in the dark. The only question was whether or not Misako would look at the date she'd left for her.

13

Unk sat around a dinner table with a family who looked as though they all came from Pete's tribe. They wore the same strange animal hides made from thin material. One of the little humans even had a giant lizard head on his chest cloth, but it was drawn like cave art. The female had wanted Unk and the male to "wash up" before dinner. They'd used a stream that the male had controlled with a lever.

It was a strange world, but Unk understood one thing, and that was turkey. The man had insisted Unk use his spice on the turkey. He had hidden a smaller fire stick in his coat, to remind Unk who was the leader. The entire family lit up with delight at Unk's creation. Even the littlest one with lizard chest cloth warmed up to Unk and gave him a hug. Unk didn't have the heart to thwack any of them by the end of the meal.

Later that night, Unk sat on the porch with the man while he smoked. The fellow had placed the fire stick on his lap. Unk wondered whether it was a ceremonial night, as back home, the tribe would only smoke on important days, such as when the moon went to bed, or the sun decided to come out for longer. There was also a beverage the man had called "beer." The liquid was yellow and smooth. Even though Unk had just met this family, the pranks were already formulating in his mind.

"Well, Unk," the man said. "It seems as though I'm in a bit of a pickle. The professor paid me to stake out that parking lot, waiting for people like you. He was even more excited to hear I got you and that Pete fella."

Unk grunted at the sound of Pete's name.

"I know. I know," the man continued and attempted to flick the flint and fire device, but the wind kept blowing it out. "I don't have him anymore, and you're pretty much worthless. But that still doesn't change the fact that the professor has my balls in a vice here. He pretty much has this whole town in a vice. You either work for the professor, or you don't work, you see, and I have this nice house. I don't like imagining my kids living in the refuse piles of those who *don't* work for the professor. So you see my predicament."

Unk grunted again. He didn't understand much of what was being said. He knew a few words here and there, just from hanging around with Pete and Clara. One of these days, Unk would have to learn more. The man stood up to light his next smoke in the corner of the porch that was shielded from the cool night breeze. Unk seized the opportunity to grab the man's "beer," and set to work on his next masterpiece.

Once the man had finally lit the firestick, he sauntered back to the chairs, unaware that Unk had manipulated the beer can. "It turns out, I hate the professor as much as the next guy, and with your spice, I think we've got a real shot at toppling that burrito empire of his. So what do you say? Do we put this whole kidnapping thing in the past, find your friend, and start ourselves a business?"

The man stuck his hand out, and Unk shook it. The caveman had learned from Pete that the sign of friendship was shaking hands, which was good, because the man was about to get it, and Unk only pranked the people he liked. The man had even forgotten his fire stick on the coffee table. He grabbed his beer, and before he lifted it, he said, "I'll tell you what, I've got a great cheese that will do any burrito right. Just wait till you try it. You'll see."

He lifted his can to toast their partnership and took a swig. He spat it out, and said, "Did you pee in my beer?"

Unk could not contain his laughter. He hooted with delight. The man laughed and slapped Unk on the back.

"You got me good!" he yelled, as they both laughed into the night.

———

Misako and Pete were dropped off at the overgrown parking lot. They'd hitched a ride from a kooky old man with Professor's Burrito Shack wrappers littering the backseat. The man had cheese drippings on his shirt, and Pete could smell the mouth-watering taste long after the burrito had been in the car. He seethed, just thinking about the burrito. He was the one who'd planned to be a rich Mexican food mogul, not this professor.

Once the car had disappeared over the hill, Misako popped her finger off and produced a flashlight. They were wandering through the desert when she stopped Pete, and said, "Something happened here!"

"What?" Pete said.

"Hang on," Misako said. In her gruff detective voice, she pushed Pete aside, and said, "Step aside, pretty boy. You're getting footprints all over my crime scene."

"How do you know it's a crime scene?"

"You doubt my investigative abilities?" Misako's eyes narrowed.

"No, I was just wondering out loud—as I sometimes do—"

Misako jumped Pete and slammed his face into the dirt. "Look at those footprints, and tell me what you see!"

"Can't you just investigate as Misako?"

"I am investigating!"

"Yeah, but don't you have less—violent—investigative techniques."

"Are you critiquing my technique?"

After spitting out a mouthful of dirt, Pete sputtered, "Um—yeah."

Misako perked up. Her face softened and brightened. Her eyes got wide, and a big grin crossed her face. "My only other investigative program is CLUEFINDER!—your friendly neighborhood sleuth. Last week, I solved the mystery of the missing baseball."

"A kid's show host?"

"We don't choose our personality programs. Now, let's get to work solving this mystery!" Misako said in a voice that if it got any higher, would shatter glass. "What do we have here? It's footprints! Can you tell me the difference between the footprints?" Misako paused and smiled.

"Um—they were made by shoes?" Pete said.

"That's right! One's bigger and the other's smaller!"

"I didn't say that—"

"By the size of the feet, one is Clara-sized! The other, a mystery man. Ooh." Misako said and made some scary noises.

"It could be a woman with really large feet."

"Women don't wear a size fifteen! Now, notice here how the tracks are evenly paced, walking together. Then here, they stop, turn, face each other. One runs. The other hesitates, and then follows. Have you got all that?"

"No."

"Good! Because we're just at the heart of the mystery! The kidnapping, and possible murder!" Misako said with children's programming gusto.

"He killed her?"

"Oh, silly dill pickle! Not here! There would be blood all over the place!"

"That's terrible."

Misako switched between her children's TV host persona, and her cop persona, then manhandled Pete, "You want me to make investigating pleasant, you've only got two choices—her way, or my way."

"Can we stop investigating now?" Pete squeaked.

"We still haven't figured out how to find her—because she was dragged into a truck! Dance break time!" Misako bounced with joy.

"Maybe we can use the time machine. She left it right there in the bushes," Pete said.

Misako danced in the parking lot where Clara was kidnapped. She stopped when Pete mentioned the time machine, and slipped back into her normal persona, "It looks as though you've figured it out, so I don't need to use my investigative subroutines anymore. But I have one question for you: How did you find it, when it was so clearly left for me to discover, via my data connection to it?"

"Um—I had to pee, so I figured while you were dancing—" Pete shrugged.

"Forget I asked. Hmm—The date on this is July 29th, 1965. It seems as though Clara has left us a message."

"Do you think she went back to that date?" Pete said.

"She couldn't. She would have had to take the time machine with her."

"So why *that* day? I mean it's not as though anything happened on that day—It was only the release date of The Beatles' song, 'Help! '"

"How did you know that?"

"Hey, I may not be smart at a lot of things, like at math, science, physics, English, gym class, computers—you know, the stuff where you have to know things—but I am good at music—and burritos. You have any music- or burrito-related investigations, I'm there. In fact, I think she chose the date so that we would think of the album *Help!*"

Misako tuned him out and muttered to herself. "The Beatles, interesting—accessing local cell towers—searching internet—ah—the Beatles' film *Help!*—a follow-up blend of song and slapstick to the hit movie, *A Hard*—"

They both slipped into their separate worlds for a brief period, while they puzzled out Clara's message that she had left behind on the time machine. At roughly the same time they both realized what it had meant, and said simultaneously, "I know what it means!"

"You first," Misako said and motioned Pete to continue.

"She needs our help."

"Is that all?"

"That's pretty much it."

"Right—I think it's more a reference to her professor. She said that she used to play the Beatles in the lab, ergo, someone she knew, who had turned on her. I assume if we find the professor, we'll find Clara."

"How are we going to do that?"

"You don't build a billion dollar burrito business, and go unnoticed."

"A billion dollars!" Pete was even more pissed than before.

"Let's see—checking the internet—from what it looks like, he lives in a giant golden mansion, built into the side of the mountain."

"I thought the mountain was national parkland."

"He lobbied to have that law revoked years ago. He needed some place to build his castle. Now come on. Let's go get Unk so that we can save Clara."

"There's no cars out here. It'll take us hours to walk back into the city."

"I believe the people of your time period call it an 'Uber.' Call one of those."

"Do they even pick you up in the middle of nowhere?"

"Of course they do. It's driver's choice, after all. There are so many fascinating things on your Internet. Your culture is wonderful. Though I'm not sure about this phenomenon you call "boy bands."

"Trust me; I'm not sure about it either. So why did we hitchhike out here? Why didn't we just call an Uber before?"

"I'm only just learning about your culture. The real question is why *you* didn't think of it."

"I make it a general policy not to think of stuff. The last time I thought of something, it was mixing everything together at a Fro Yo shop, and it didn't taste very good."

"We'll need to start thinking now. I do believe I've found out where the professor has taken Clara." Misako held out her palm, and a holographic display appeared. It displayed an *Albuquerque Journal* article about the professor taking a wife. Clara was pictured being brought into a giant house by the professor. However, her expression was more terror than excitement for wedding nuptials. "According to the article," Misako continued, "the ceremony is to take place tomorrow, but this picture was taken at his estate up in the mountains."

Misako flicked through several screens until she got to an exterior view of the estate. Pete's eyes widened when he saw where it was.

"I know where that is!" Pete said. "It's in this rich neighborhood that's right up against the mountain. I know, because my friend Tito and I used to take his herbal supplements there."

"Like echinacea goldenseal?"

"Is that one of Snoop Dogg's?"

"Nevermind. Does that mean you know someone who lives there? Maybe we can—" Misako asked.

"Oh, no, you see that gate? That used to be where the parking lot was, and where the mansion's located used to be a national park. We used to climb the boulders until we saw some sweet view of the city."

Headlights appeared on the road. Misako said, "That's the Uber; come on. Let's go."

———

Aside from forced at gunpoint, the professor treated Clara like a princess. They drove up to a large gate leading up to the side of the mountain far from the Sandia Man Cave. The road led to a golden monstrosity built into the mountain's edge. Pillars framed the massive front door as if a Roman emperor had decided to rule over Albuquerque.

The professor brought the SUV to a halt in front of the door, and a slew of servants flooded from the entrance. He motioned with the gun for Clara to get out of the car, and a servant took her by the hand to help her. The professor stashed the gun in the glove compartment and got out. A rabble of press camped outside his house took pictures, and their questions jumbled in a sea of voices. Before Clara could think about talking to the press, she noticed two bald hulking men, who probably went by the name of Brick and Pork Chop, stepped in between her and the reporters.

A woman with a pencil skirt and thick glasses, holding three smartphones, approached Clara as she was shuffled towards the doorway. "I'm so happy to meet you. My name's Nadine, and I'll be your personal assistant." She stuck her hand out.

Clara awkwardly shook her hand and was given a smart phone. Clara swiped at the screen, but it was locked. Before Clara could say anything, Nadine led Clara through the giant maze of a house. It was more grand and garish than a Vegas hotel, and servants were at every corner. The two large men trailed behind her, keeping their distance, but still within a range to prevent any plans she might hatch to escape. Her new-found personal assistant saw her looking at the men and said, "They're here for your protection. There are lots of crazy people out there you know."

"—like the one who kidnapped me."

Nadine looked around and lowered her voice, "Hey, look, I know it's a bit of a shock, but it could be worse."

"'Could be worse?' I suppose a shark could attack me while deep sea diving!"

"See, that's the spirit. Now let me show you to your room," Nadine said and shuffled Clara into a room. It looked like the suite of a princess more than the prison cell she'd expected. There was a four-poster bed that was of a very old and ornate design. On the bed was something that made her heart stop. It was a wedding dress.

Nadine nodded to the beefy men, and they stood outside the door. She shut the door, and it turned with a click. She turned, and Clara was already looking for a way out. There were no other exits from the room, except for a bathroom. There was a balcony. However, it offered a breathtaking view of Albuquerque and a life-taking dive off a cliff. The bride-to-be glanced at the smartphone she'd been given, and attempted to unlock it. The word "PIN" appeared on the screen.

"Give me the PIN," Clara demanded.

"Why?" Nadine said.

"Because I'm calling the police."

"I wouldn't do that."

"Why?"

"The professor owns the police."

"Well, the FBI then; I don't care."

"Look," Nadine said. "I'll unlock it for you, but the professor runs this town. He's greased all the right palms, and your call won't make it to the right people. Like it or not, you're stuck here, honey. It really could be worse. It's not every day that the professor picks a wife."

"I am not marrying that man!"

"Lower your voice!"

"I don't see how I can make it any worse."

"There are women who would kill to be in your position. Besides, just because you're his wife, doesn't mean you can't have a lover on the side."

Nadine made a move, and Clara jumped back.

"I'm not that kind of girl!" Clara yelled.

Scorned, Nadine tossed the cell phone on the floor, and said, "Fine, have it your way. I'll give you the unlock code when you can listen to reason."

Nadine turned to leave and slammed the door. Clara banged on the doorway to no avail. The muffled voice of one of the meat sticks called through the doorway, and said, "Look, lady, if you want to jump, go ahead and do it. He'll collect the insurance policy, and save us the headache of listening to you."

Clara roared and kicked the door a few times. She stomped over to the bed, tore the dress from its spot, and threw it on the ground. She stepped on it a few times for good measure and sat on the bed.

After a moment, she saw the cell phone on the floor and picked it up. She tried all the codes that came to mind and even ones that were long shots. It was a slow, tedious process. She would get five attempts. The phone would lock for thirty seconds, and then she would get five more. As a graduate student, she was used to slow, tedious processes. Code a time jump. Run the simulations. Record the results. Code again.

It was the same now. Enter all the dates important to the professor: his tenure date, the publication of his papers, the day he'd thought of how to break the time barrier, etc. Each iteration of numbers would result in a locked phone, but eventually, she would stumble on something. There was a series of four numbers out there. She just had to find it.

———

The same kooky old man with the burrito wrappers in the back seat picked them up from the forgotten parking lot. While they were driving back towards Albuquerque, and making their way to the Northeast Heights, Pete asked the man, "So if you're an Uber driver, why'd you pick us up as hitchhikers before?"

The man smiled, and hooted, "'Cause I just like driving people. I don't care if you're a hitchhiker or not."

"Yeah, but you could get paid for it."

"What if you couldn't pay for it? You think I'll just leave someone who needs a ride, just because they don't have any money?"

They wove through the neighborhoods at the foot of the mountain. As the roads became steeper, the houses became nicer and nicer, until they reached the garish arches of the professor's estate.

"Yeah, but you get paid to drive—" Pete said. He didn't understand the man. As a business owner, Pete would give out free samples, but not an entire burrito. If somebody were hungry and didn't have the money, they would have to go somewhere else. Pete couldn't feed the entire city of Albuquerque.

"Look," the man said. "You sometimes do something, not because it will make you money, but because it's right. Now, that will be $234.35."

"Two hundred dollars!" Pete yelped.

"I did drive you from the middle of nowhere," the man said.

"We've already paid by the app," Misako said.

"Still, two hundred dollars—" Pete said as he climbed out of the car. While they watched the taillights speed away, Pete had an afterthought, "Wait, Misako. How did you pay for it? You don't have any money."

"I used your bank account," Misako said. "It was simple to hack because you write down all your passwords, and in the background of a photo at a party in your house, right behind Tito's left elbow, is the password list. If you zoom in close enough and enhance the image with extrapolative data, your passwords are quite visible. Don't worry. I've smudged and reuploaded the photo to prevent further tampering."

"But I need that money! I have to buy ingredients."

"I don't think anyone will be buying your burritos in this time period," Misako said and looked back towards the city. Even from the gate of the mansion, they could see the city spread out beneath them. It was the same Albuquerque Pete knew well, except for the golden pillars glittering in the night.

Pete wrung his hands, and said, "Let's get this jerkhole."

"Great. First, we have to get inside."

One of the press camped outside snorted, and said, "Good luck with that! Official wedding business only—and you don't look so official to me."

"How do you know we aren't?" Misako huffed and pressed a button on the side.

A sleepy security guard answered, "Yeah, what do you want?"

"Yeah, um—" Pete said. "We're here for official wedding business."

"It's midnight, man! Plus the wedding is tomorrow."

"We have an important delivery," Misako said. "The professor needs it by tonight."

A camera shifted on the gate, "I don't see your delivery truck. Where did you say you were from, again?"

Pete thought quickly. "Neil Lane." He might not know a lot of things, but he did know his reality TV. The Bachelor used Neil Lane for all their engagement rings, and if a person were going to buy a wedding ring for a person, they'd practically just met, then it might as well be a Neil Lane.

"Hah! See, now I know you're lying! The wedding rings are coming from Fingerhut!" the guard said triumphantly.

Misako stepped up, with her tough voice, and said, "Listen here; you want to go interrupt the professor's bachelor party because you're about to turn away his rings on the night before his wedding, be my guest. The other option is, you pause whatever you're watching on Netflix, get your ass out of your booth, and come pick up the package. You don't have to let us in, for us to get you this package."

"Uh—be right there—" The owner of the voice clicked off the speaker.

Pete said, "That was awesome. However, unless you have a wedding ring, I don't see how this will help."

"You've never really infiltrated billionaire's houses before, have you?" Misako said.

"I've never done anything before. I mean, aside from time travel. I haven't even ever left Albuquerque."

"Well, to be fair, I haven't infiltrated billionaire's houses either, but I *have* worked on a lot of cases involving them, and if there's one thing you can count on for just about every billionaire's household—."

The gate opened, and a pudgy security guard stepped out. Misako punched him in the face, and he went down with one punch. Before the press could converge on them, they dragged the security inside and closed the gates. Misako began stripping the man of his uniform, and continued to talk, "—there are so many staff members, that often the left hand doesn't know what the right is doing. Now, put on this man's clothes."

She tossed a shirt in Pete's face. It smelled like loneliness and loss.

14

After what seemed like hours, Clara had finally unlocked the phone. The perv had bought her a phone, and used *her* PIN code on it, which meant that her professor had *known* her PIN code. All the times she had thought she had lost her phone in the lab, he had probably nicked it and downloaded the pictures on her phone to his personal collection. She could not believe that man.

She was about to dial the police when she had a second thought. She was in an altered reality, no doubt, where he'd abused time travel for his advantage. If that was the case, there was no telling how much he had changed. If he'd decided to go back to the drafting of the Constitution of the United States, he might be more than just some rich jerkbox with enough money to make officials turn the other way. She couldn't trust anyone in this timeline.

As much as Pete bumbled around, she knew he would do the right thing. She dialed Pete's cell phone number. After a few rings, she got through. Misako answered, "Hello?"

"Misako?" Clara said.

"Oh, hey."

"Are you with Pete?"

"Not at the moment. We split up to cover more ground. I hacked into his wireless carrier, and spoofed his phone, using my networking hardware. I figured it would be good to have access to a phone line, in case you tried to call."

"Here I am, and get me out of here!"

"We're attempting to find your location. Pete is dressed as a security guard, and I'm dressed as a maid. This house is massive."

"I don't know where I am, but there are two goons outside the door."

"Just keep your connection open. I'm a police bot too. I can run traces on your phone number."

"Hurry; he wants to marry me."

"That upsets me. I want to marry you."

"I'm flattered. I really am. However, let's start with a cup of coffee first."

"Your marriage rituals involve coffee. I didn't read that on Wikipedia."

"No, I mean, let's start with a date. What do you mean, Wikipedia?"

"I just read the entirety of Wikipedia on the way over. I figured I should get to know your culture a little bit."

She found herself a little turned on by that. She liked women who were voracious readers. Most of her first girlfriends, she'd met on Goodreads. Before she could say another word, she heard the latch on the door turn. She kicked the phone under the bed, and could hear Misako's voice, "Hello? Hello?" fade away.

The professor stumbled into the room. It was evident that he'd had a little too much to drink, as he fumbled towards her with his arms out. She side-stepped him, and he face planted onto the bed.

"Isn't it unlucky to see the bride on the night before her wedding?" Clara said.

The professor flopped over, and said, "The guys at the bachelor party. They brought this girl over, but while she was dancing—I just couldn't stop thinking about you."

As much as she was grossed out by his behavior, she was in a precarious situation and controlled her urge to eviscerate him verbally. "We have a professional relationship, and that's all."

"But can't it be more? You're the only one who understands me. The jerks at UNM only pretend to like me because I bring in research dollars. The undergrads hate my class. I look forward to spending nights in the lab with you." The professor pouted.

"Ethical considerations aside, it's not even a possibility. I'm not sexually attracted to men."

"I know you probably made that decision because some guy burned you long ago—"

"It's not a decision! I was born this way."

"Yeah, but aren't all gays bisexual?"

"Not everyone is—" Clara said, and was about to lose control, but decided to back off. If she could play the situation right, maybe she could get some information out of him, such as what he did to the timeline. She sat next to him on the bed. "Look, you're a brilliant scientist, and I came to get my Ph.D. because you were one of the faculty I wanted to work with."

She wasn't lying to him. She *had* wanted to work with him. She just didn't know he'd be so difficult to work with, until halfway through her Ph.D. At that point, she'd decided to stick it out, and see it through. She would be leaving Albuquerque anyway, after her graduate work. Pretty much no one in higher education stayed at where they'd completed their Ph.D., at least in the career track she was aiming for.

"So why don't we just keep it professional for now," Clara said, and he sat up. She could smell the alcohol on his breath. Before he could make any moves on her, she asked him a question she knew he'd answer. He had a large ego and could be diverted with a little stroking of it. "So tell me how you did it. It's pretty amazing if you ask me."

"Did what?" The professor wobbled back and forth on the bed.

"All of this. I figure you got this through time travel. Maybe a sports almanac, or something?"

"What?" The professor said and then laughed. "Oh, no, no, I was just as stuck as the rest of you."

"Wait? You were there with us? Pete said you had died!"

"No, that idiot you hang out with just *thought* I'd died when I'd slipped into unconsciousness. When I came to, I ran back into the lab, and there was just a time vortex."

"So you jumped in?"

"I was trying to save you."

"So why didn't you approach us?"

"I did several times, but each time that Neanderthal got in the way. I stepped to the right, and he would step in front of me, then I'd go left, and he would be there. One time, I tried to sneak in at night, and he threatened me with a club. He's quite protective of you."

"Unk may be a giant ball of muscle, but he has a good heart."

"You named him?"

Clara shrugged and said. "So how did you get back here?"

"I didn't. I snuck into the deep recesses of the cave when you were all out, and just waited for you to fix the machine. You were doing a brilliant job. I figured I would just step in when you traveled back, but then when we got into that future, you were all arrested, so I hid in the back of the cave again. Before I could make any reasonable plans, you had all made it back. I was about to approach you when I heard that robot mention something about how there were portable time travel devices in that world. Think about it! Such a device would be amazing! I couldn't go back with you, so I stayed behind. I got one of my own!"

The professor pulled out a phone from his pocket.

"You got a smartphone?" Clara asked, confused.

"No, this is my phone. I just downloaded the time travel app from that alternate future."

"You can time travel with an app?"

"It's great! I can travel anywhere! I was going to go back and show you when I got this idea. I figured that you would be traveling back to the same time as the night of the lab experiment, and since I have a time machine, I figured I'd make myself a billionaire. You'd have to love me then."

"You think I'd love you because you were rich?"

"Of course; don't all women want a rich man to take care of them?" The professor leaned in for a kiss, and Clara backed away. He grabbed her and forced his lips on hers. She punched him in the balls and jumped off the bed.

He collapsed to the floor and yelled, "Fine; you want to do this the hard way! You stupid bitch, you *will* marry me. Or else, I'll have your family killed."

"You wouldn't," Clara said.

The professor swiped his phone. He pulled up a security feed of his house. Clara saw her parents sleeping in a guest room. It looked a lot like the room that they were in. The professor typed a command into his phone, and a person dressed all in black tiptoed into the room. They pulled out a gun with a silencer.

"OK! I'll do it," Clara said, tears streaming down her eyes. "Just leave my mum and dad out of it."

The professor hit another command, and the assassin retreated. "Good, now that we have this understanding. Your parents are very excited to be seeing you tomorrow, and trust me. Should anything go wrong at the wedding, or even on our honeymoon, you would not believe what money can buy."

"What has become of you?"

"It was always there, honey. You just bring out the best in me. Now get some sleep. We have a big day tomorrow." He cupped her chin and kissed her forehead.

As soon as he was out of the room, she dove under the bed for the phone. She pulled it out, and said, "Misako. Are you there?"

"Yeah. What happened?" Misako said.

"Please, hurry," Clara said, and turned around. She jumped to see the professor standing there. He had the two goons behind him. He

- 92 -

nodded; one of the goons grabbed the phone from Clara and crushed it with his fist.

"I stole a robot from the alternate timeline too," he said and grinned. "Well, actually two. I figured I needed something that could keep up with that toy bot of yours."

––––––––

Pete, wearing security guard clothes, found that no one bothered to stop him as he wandered through the house. It didn't take long to discover a kitchen. It wasn't just any kitchen, but the test kitchen for the professor's burritos. It was all the secrets to success. Clara wasn't going anywhere till morning, so Pete figured maybe he could learn a thing or two.

He made his way to a fridge that was set apart from the rest. It was labeled "THE NEXT BIG THING." Inside was a plate with the best burrito Pete had ever seen in his life. The tortilla was mouth-wateringly perfect. The garnish was expertly designed. It looked delicious.

There were containers of the different ingredients, on the other shelves in the fridge, that included eggs, potatoes, bacon, green chile, and all the ingredients to make the perfect breakfast burrito. One of the containers was labeled "caveman spice." Pete opened the container and dipped his finger inside. He licked the mixture off his finger and knew the taste. Unk's spice! The professor had stolen it!

There was a set of preparation instructions, for the wedding caterer, for the day of the wedding. The professor had planned to release his new burrito at the reception. Not only had he stolen Pete's idea, but he had his recipe as well—and soon the entire world would think it was the next big creation.

Pete grabbed the prep instructions and the ingredients. He began to prepare them. He was upset and slammed the stuff around while he worked. He clicked the gas stove on and put pans on the burners. The professor had taken everything from him. Pete had to face it. His burritos were awful, his food cart a joke. If his burritos were any good, he would be the billionaire. He was about to cook when Misako burst into the room. He jumped back and dropped an egg on the floor.

"Come on! We must save Clara!" Misako yelled, then looked at all the ingredients spread on the table, and the gas flame flickering under the pans. "What are you doing?"

"The professor! He stole my idea. So I figured I'd steal it back, and learn how to make the perfect burrito." Pete said.

"Is that what you want? To be known for another man's burrito?"

"No—"

"So why are you shoving the professor's recipe into your pocket? Look, Pete, a burrito is just an extension of the person making it. You can follow a recipe to the letter, but is that you? Food is an art form. While anyone can make a burrito, only Pete can make a Pete's burrito."

Pete placed the recipe back on the countertop.

Misako grinned, and said, "Good! Let's go save Clara!"

She charged out of the room. Pete hesitated a moment before following her. He scooped up the professor's recipe, and some of the "caveman spice," stuffed them in his pocket, then dashed out of the room.

———

Pete and Misako ran down the hallway to the last known location of the phone, before the signal cut off. There were no goons guarding the doorway. When they burst into the room, no one was there. However, there were signs of a struggle, and the shards of the phone were still on the floor. The balcony's door was ajar, but no one was on the balcony.

"Where is she?" Pete yelled.

"I don't know. This is her last known location. However, she couldn't have gotten far." Misako added.

Before they were able to think of another plan, they heard a noise coming from the balcony. It was the sound of a helicopter starting its engine. The blades cut through the crisp night air in an unmistakable whomp, whomp, whomp. They ran to the balcony and looked up. On the roof, they could see the tail of a chopper sticking out.

"He's trying to escape!" Pete yelled.

Just as Pete had the thought, the door to the room flew off its hinges and crushed the four-poster bed. The two robotic goons stepped through the entrance. Misako's eyes went red. "Police Brutality setting activated."

"There's a Police Brutality setting?" Pete said.

"Get to the roof!" she yelled.

"How?" Pete said. "Those guys are blocking the way."

The goons walked toward the balcony, cracking their knuckles and necks. They shed their shirts, in anticipation of a fight.

"The distance from here to the roof is traversable with only a 17% chance of an experienced climber falling to their doom."

"What about an inexperienced climber? We had to invent a pulley just to get me up to the cave."

"Aww—hell," Misako said, and she grabbed Pete by his shirt. She thrust him over the ledge. He screamed as he saw the great abyss below.

"Wait! What are you doing?" Pete yelled and flailed about.

"Just remember to tuck and roll when you land," Misako said.

"Land? What do you mean, land?" Pete yelped, but it was too late. With a mighty swing of her arm, she launched Pete towards the roof.

The goons charged. She turned towards them.

Pete flew through the air, and his arms fluttered wildly. The pinpricks of light that were Albuquerque grew distant. Time seemed to slow down, as he heard the whomp, whomp, whomp of the chopper. The rush of wind muffled his scream, as he flew through the atmosphere.

———

Misako collided with the two bots with a thunderous clash. They both attempted to meet her charge with their fists. At the last moment, she fell backward on her hands and pushed her legs off the floor. They flew past her, and she connected her feet to their backs. They stumbled forward, dangerously close to the edge. She whirled around, with another kick to the face of one of the bots. However, he grabbed her by the leg and thrust her to the ground. The other came in to pound her, but she used the momentum of her going down to sweep the second bot off his feet.

She jerked her leg out of the clutches of the first and steadied herself. She stomped on the head of the one on the floor. It sparked, and thrashed, as wires and circuits blew in all directions. The other bot's eyes went red, and he charged her. They exchanged a series of blows as her opponent went into overdrive.

Misako backed into a corner as the machine drew closer.

———

Pete tumbled onto the roof and hit an HVAC unit. His lungs and muscles cried out in pain. The helicopter blades seemed to whir in slow motion. Whomp. Whomp. Whomp. Pete rolled over onto his side and looked up towards the helipad. He was out of breath and shaking from the terror of being tossed through the air at the edge of a cliff.

Pete forced himself to look up towards the copter. Clara was in the back, handcuffed to one of the seats. The professor was in the pilot seat, wearing a headset. He smiled at Pete and gave him a salute. He turned back to the controls and lifted the chopper into the air.

In a last burst of adrenaline, Pete forced himself to his feet and ran towards the helicopter. The machine lifted into the air, and Pete jumped towards the skids. Everything seemed to go into slow motion. Whomp. Whomp. Whomp. A tear came down Clara's eye. The copter spun towards the city.

Pete connected with the skid and held on. The chopper left the safety of the roof, heading into the chasm, and it was too much. Pete wasn't able to hold on. His hand slipped, and he plummeted towards the black earth below.

———

Once Misako had defeated the first robot, the second one fought harder. For every move she'd make, the bot would counter. Each time she kicked, he would block her. When she punched, her hands would be thrust out of the way. They had circled through the room, breaking every piece of furniture.

Misako surmised that they had had orders to bring her in alive, but when she had smashed the first robot, she'd awakened a defense protocol, and all bets were off. Each strike of the robot was meant to be a killing shot, and she had a hard time keeping up.

After a few moments of stalemate that seemed to last an eternity, she maneuvered the robot out onto the balcony. They were exchanging a series of blows when she heard the chopper take off. She saw Pete slipping from the skid.

Misako whirled around, so her back was at the balcony edge. Her opponent attempted to exploit an opening she'd purposely left, and tried to push her over. He thrust forward with two open palms. She grabbed him by the wrists and flipped him over the rail. She then flipped herself and planted both her feet on the falling bot. She jumped away, on an intercept course for Pete.

She connected with Pete in midair and plucked him from the sky. She streamlined herself to turn them back towards the cliff's edge. She thrust her fist into the cliff's edge, and they skidded to a halt, as her arm tore through the rock the way a pirate's dagger would tear through a sail, as the hero descended to the deck below.

Once they hit the ground with enough force to send Pete rolling and cause sparks to shoot forth from Misako's legs, they both spent a few moments in shock. Pete had landed in a pile of the robot goon's parts. He stumbled backward and turned to Misako. Her arm was a jumbled mess. All the artificial skin was gone, and what was left, was more a slag of scrap metal, than an arm. Her legs were also on the fritz, as she walked funny.

Pete held her as she stumbled to the ground under a piñon tree. They were in the foothills of the mountain, the last bit of wilderness before the city. Medical attention wouldn't be far away, but Pete didn't even know what he could do for her.

"It's OK," Misako said. Her voice processor was full of static. "I'm sure Clara can repair me. She's a smart woman."

"He got away," Pete said. "He took off with Clara on the copter."

"That's OK," Misako said. "I think I've figured out a way to beat him."

"How?" Pete said. "He'll be expecting us now. Security at his wedding will be tighter than ever."

"That's easy," Misako said. "We have a time machine."

"We can go back and stop him from getting the drop on Clara!" Pete said.

"Not so fast. The professor will know that we have a time machine and would have taken precautions. There's also the risk of running into ourselves."

"Because of some universe-destroying paradox?"

"Have you seen my hair? I wouldn't want to subject myself to that!"

"You did just fall down a cliff, you know."

"Is that the excuse you use for every bad hair day? Besides, there's a point in history where we can stop the professor from coming into power in the first place—"

"When?" Pete said.

"—back when he made his first small fortune: the great Burrito Cook-Off of '72."

"You're saying we go knock him out of the past, and none of this ever happened?"

"He started the Burrito Shacks with the prize money. Then after his corporation became successful, he disappeared in 1976, and let it run itself, presumably to jump forward to today when he returned from his "long sabbatical." Everything we see here was built from his instructions that were left in '76. If he doesn't win that Burrito Cook-Off, then he's not a billionaire."

"Then what happens to Clara?" Pete said.

"Time resets around her," Misako said.

"So wait," Pete said. "If we go back and change the past, it will just change around Clara and the professor?"

"Yes," Misako said. "They're tethered to the time travel device. The world will simply cease to be what it is, and become what we change. Clara and the professor will be the only witnesses to it. It's the same reason I didn't disappear when we changed the timeline where I came from. It locks your timeline in place, so you don't disappear if you kill your grandfather or something."

"Who would want to kill their grandfather?"

"Adolf Hitler the III."

"Who would name their kid Adolf Hitler?"

"Let's just go to the Burrito Cook-Off."

"Great! Let's do it. You should beat him, no problem."

Misako looked at her broken arm, and then back up at Pete. "I'm not going to be winning any competitions with this arm."

"But—" Pete said.

"Remember Pete; the burrito is in you."

"I guess."

"You'd better do more than guess. Luckily, we have time. I figure we can do a jump back a couple of months before the competition, to give you some training."

"But—"

"Hey, let's not forget Unk. You'll be needing his spice. From the security logs, I know exactly where he's being held."

15

Misako and Pete made their way to a house not too far from the mansion. It looked like a typical suburban place, in a typical suburban neighborhood—but that didn't change the fact that the man inside had shoot-to-kill orders for both Unk and Pete. The professor had sent out the go-ahead to take out the hostages, once he'd escaped with Clara.

Since Misako had the security guard's access, she was able to monitor all security communications coming to and from the mansion. She'd intercepted the transmission to kill off Unk, and anyone that tried to save him. However, that was only when the professor was in the mansion. Once he was out of the vicinity and was no longer using the mansion's security network, all bets were off. There was no guarantee that the professor wouldn't call back, or worse, that the person in this house would phone out when they hadn't heard anything.

Misako and Pete approached with caution. There were lights on in the living room and some commotion. Pete could see Unk's shadow through the curtains. His mane of wild hair was hard to miss. From the looks of it, he was being tortured. He was thrashing around, while two assailants assaulted him.

Misako and Pete nodded to each other. Even though Misako was in no condition to fight, she was still super-strong, and bullet resistant. Pete had the gun he'd liberated from the security guard. They figured their best option was to come in hard and fast, to scare the men into submission. They tiptoed to the front window.

Pete nodded and turned his face for a second. Misako used her mangled arm to shatter the front window. Pete charged in with the gun, and Misako jumped in with him. She was unarmed, but more than a match for any human. They screamed orders for everyone to get on the ground.

What they saw was unexpected. Unk had been wrestling while two small children giggled. They cowered behind Unk, in fear of the people who had just crashed through their window. The man who'd abducted Pete was on the couch, reaching for his gun, but Misako had stepped on his hand with a crunch.

His wife, who had been playing a game on a tablet, screamed at the both of them, "What the hell are you doing!"

"Um—We're here to save our friend," Pete said.

"I'll have you know, Unk is a guest in our house!"

"You kidnapped him!" Pete said.

The man reaching for the gun cradled his broken hand. He said, "That was the plan at first. But look at the guy. Unk's such a great guy—and his pranks–Believe you me; I never laughed so hard in my life. The piss in the beer gag! It's a classic!"

"You're letting him go?" Pete said.

"I was going to let him go with my secret homemade cheese, to help you take down that rat bastard professor, but since you broke my window—"

"—and your hand," the wife added.

"—and my hand," the man said, "I think I'm going to let you off with nothing."

"You have cheese that could help us?" Pete said.

"Hell, yeah," the man said. "Come on down to my basement. I call it Cheesoria."

"There he goes again," the wife said. "Get him talking about that damned cheese, and he'll never shut up."

———————

The man shooed Pete and Misako downstairs. Unk continued to play with the children, upstairs. They entered an entire cheese-making operation in the basement of the man's house. There were shelves and shelves full of various wheels of cheeses. The man sliced some of his cheese and handed it to Pete.

"Look, if you don't trust me." The man ate the slice, gave another to Pete and a third to Misako.

The slice was the most exquisite cheese Pete had ever tasted. Better yet, it tasted as though it would blend perfectly with Misako's egg recipe and Unk's spice. If there were a cheese served in heaven, this would be the cheese. Unfortunately, the only place this man would be serving it was in hell. While they were distracted by pure deliciousness, the man pulled out a shotgun he'd hidden away. He used his broken hand as a prop for the gun.

"Now," the man said. "While your boy Unk, here, might be an asset to the family business, and a good friend, you two are disposable. Now, any business needs capital to get started and let's say that the professor is offering a big bonus for the bodies of both of you. I'd imagine he'd forget about Unk if I show him the bodies of you two."

"You'd do this in front of your kids?" Misako said. "Even the Mob doesn't off somebody in front of their kids!"

"Oh, don't you play Miss Perfect with me," the man said. "You know the world's gone to hell. The rich get richer and do whatever they want. We're left to fight for scraps. Besides, my wife is putting them to bed right about now, thanks to Unk, for tiring the little shits out. I'll clean the basement before morning."

"What about Unk?" Pete said. "He won't let you do this."

"Unk's a cretin! As much as I love him, he's more of a dog than a human. His caveman brain is the size of a walnut. He'll follow anyone who throws food at him."

"I think he's smarter than you give him credit for. I think he'd do just as well as I would on a math test, and I'm not very good at math!"

"I don't think that's a compliment," Misako said.

"The point is," Pete said. "He's standing right behind you."

Pete pointed behind the man. Unk raised a giant cheese wheel and thwacked the gun-toting cheesemaker alongside the head. The fellow was out in one hit. Unk laughed and patted Pete on the shoulder. "Hey, buddy," Pete said. "I missed you, too."

"Come on," Misako said. "We have to get to a safe place to time travel. Unless you want to end up in this basement in the Seventies, which could be solid earth then, for all we know."

"Wait," Pete said. "What about the cheese? This is the best cheese I've ever tasted."

"Take a wheel," Misako said. "If the competition allows us to bring our own ingredients, then it might be useful."

"What about beyond that?" Pete said.

"I don't follow," Misako said.

"I mean, the only way to beat the professor at his game, is to perfect the ultimate burrito before him. Otherwise, he'll just time travel back, and invent the burrito in a different era. We'll need enough cheese to do whatever it takes."

"That's a good point."

"Good, so what I'm thinking is that we'll travel back to five years ago. I'll befriend this man. Maybe I'll show up at his door dressed in nothing but rags, and tell him I'm here to apprentice with him in the ancient art of cheese making. He'll ignore me at first, but I'll wait in the cold, the rain, and the snow. Then days later, when he realizes I'm serious, he'll teach me his ways, and then—."

"Or you could just take the recipe he stapled right here."
Misako pointed to a sheet on the wall.

"Um—that too—" Pete said.

"Besides, you don't even need to do that. To stop the professor, we just need to smash his time travel device after we win the Cook-Off. He'll no longer be protected from the flow of time. It should be easy when he has no goons at his side. Now, come on!" Misako said and charged out of the basement. Unk took a cheese wheel and ran up the stairs.

Pete looked around for a moment or two. Then he grabbed the recipe from the wall and stuffed it into his pocket.

——————

The only place that was safe for time travel was on the outskirts of town. Inside the city, they couldn't be sure if there would be witnesses. Considering that a left-over pulley had completely altered the course of human history, they had to be careful going into the past. Once they were in the desert that surrounded the city, they found a point where the hills surrounding them would shield them from onlookers. Misako opened a portal and stepped through. The others followed.

On the other side, Pete ate a mouthful of dirt. No matter how many times he'd traveled through the fabric of time, he always landed at an awkward angle. From the heat on his back, and light shining in his eyes, Pete could tell it was daylight. Before Pete could collect himself, Unk waved his hands and pointed in fear. Up ahead, on a hill, was a man on a warhorse. He was wearing full Spanish plate mail and had a mount adorned with steel. No wonder the Aztecs had thought Cortez was a half-man, half-horse being. The armor of the man almost blended with the armor of the horse.

"Calm down!" Pete said. "You'll alert him to our presence! Misako, what date did you enter into the—"

Pete looked around, but Misako wasn't anywhere to be seen.

The rider saw them and spurred his horse into a gallop. Unk stepped backwards and ran. Pete stumbled after Unk, but couldn't keep up.

"Wait!" Pete cried out.

Unk disappeared over the hill, and Pete had run only a few feet before the rider caught up to him. He heard the whoosh of air, and a bolas entangled his feet. He crashed face first into the ground. Pete heard the hoofs circle him a few times before the rider dismounted. Just as Pete was about to turn over, he heard the unmistakable sound of a sword being unsheathed.

"Don't stab me!" Pete said. "I don't have proper health insurance. I tried to get some, but there were too many choices."

"On your feet, English pig," a voice with a Spanish accent demanded.

Pete lifted himself up to his feet. The man was wearing a conquistador helmet exactly as Pete had seen in his history books. Pete remembered his teacher telling them about how some guy named Coronado pillaged through New Mexico looking for the Seven Cities of Gold. If that guy had only come 470 years later, he could have gone to the Cities of Gold casino.

"I'm not English. My last name is Jaramillo," Pete responded to the man.

"So, you're a spy, then!" The man pressed his sword against Pete's throat.

"My friend Tito and I tried to break into the ladies locker room once. It was Tito's idea. He thought if we wore towels on our heads, and put on mudpacks, with cucumbers on our eyes, no would notice that we weren't girls, but we didn't even get to the entrance. It was hard to walk with cucumbers taped to our eyes, and when the coach saw us—"

"Enough!" The man pressed the sword, and a bead of blood appeared on the tip.

"Sorry, I have a tendency to talk, when I get nervous."

"Where is your conspirator? English pig! Tell me this, and I'll let you live."

"I'm telling you; I'm not English! I'm mostly Spanish."

"So why do you not speak it?"

"I don't know. I just never learned it. I wasn't good at foreign languages in school."

"Hah! So you admit, you *are* English! Did you come here to spy on me? Are you here to find the Seven Cities of Cibola?"

"Wait—Are you, Coronado?"

"Francisco Vázquez de Coronado y Luján."

"Dude! You have a mall named after you."

"Is this mall grand?"

"Oh, yeah. It has Abercrombie *and* Fitch."

"Do they have stately processions at this mall?"

"One time, I saw Hootie and the Blowfish play a Green Chile Fest in the parking lot."

"Do the great families pay their respect?"

"I think they had a clown-face painting booth for the kids if I recall—"

"What? You let children masquerade around in a mall named after me! You English scum have gone too far!"

Coronado pulled some rope from his horse and bound Pete's hands. When the prisoner struggled and tried to break free, the man threw him to the ground, and Pete ate a face full of dirt for the second time that day.

———

Misako tumbled out of the portal, onto the ground, and rolled to her feet. She was getting the hang of time travel. Even though her arm was mangled, she'd repaired most of the circuitry in her legs. Most of her systems self-repaired certain types of damage. If she'd been in her own time period, she would have just gotten a replacement of stuff she couldn't auto-repair. Now she just had to hope that Clara was as good an engineer, as she was a physicist.

She turned around to talk to Pete, but he wasn't there. Since her tracks were the only disturbance in the sand, she had to figure that Pete and Unk hadn't made it. She pulled up the command screen of the device, to see if they had gone through when she noticed something funny. The time coordinates had a fork programmed into them. The first time was the one she'd programmed. It was set to '72. The other was set to 1542. From what she could deduce, it was programmed to let one person through, and dump the rest back in time.

She programmed the device to go back to 1542, plus an hour, to avoid landing on top of Pete, so she could pick them up when she heard a voice behind her. It was the professor. "I wouldn't do that if I were you."

Misako turned around to see him holding a gun, while his two robot goons stood behind him. They were undamaged by their scuffle in the future, and the professor looked ten years younger. This must be the version of him that was about to enter the cooking competition. It was the one who had just traveled from her time period to hatch his plan.

The two goons walked towards Misako, and she had a choice to make. She had beaten them in combat once before, however, when she'd fought them the first time, it had been in the future. If she fought now, would they use their knowledge of her, the second time they encountered her? She was also damaged and had barely beaten them with two good arms. Instead, she hoped that Pete would do what any traveler knows to do, if they get separated, and go back to the point where it happened. She hit the time travel button and tossed the machine up into the air. The vortex appeared above them and sucked the device into it.

The two goons tackled her, but it was too late. The device was already on its journey to 1542. They subdued her very quickly and forced her to her feet. The professor walked over to her, and said, "You know, I thought it would be Clara who'd travel through. Otherwise, I would have just stranded you all."

"You're the one who programmed the split in the time vortex!" Misako said.

"Well, duh," the professor explained. "I mean, I needed insurance, should you try to travel back in time to stop me. You're the only other people with a time machine, so when everyone was gone from the cave one day, I reprogrammed the interface. If you ever traveled to 1972, it would let the controller of the device through, then the split in the portal would toss the others back into 1542. It was a pretty violent time back then, and the Spanish didn't get along very well with English-speaking folks. I figured, why off you when history could do it for me."

It had occurred to Misako that this professor didn't know he had Clara in his wedding trap in the future. If this were the past version of the professor, then his plans were just forming, and he most likely thought that the group was still together. If there were one advantage she had over him, it was his love for Clara. "So what now; you're just going to risk Clara being killed in the past?"

The professor got angry. "I didn't plan to kill Clara! I programmed it to let the controller make it to here, and alert me when she got here. I figured that it would be her! Who would have thought she'd have programmed her bot to use this complicated piece of machinery!" He cradled his time travel unit.

She had two advantages over him. He also underestimated her. While the models he'd plucked from the future were nothing more than glorified toasters, she was a self-aware and learning artificial intelligence. She needed to be smart, to be a lawyer, cop, therapist, and television entourage in one unit. However, she'd encountered the prejudice before. Most humans of her era thought that because she'd been programmed, rather than having been born, that she was nothing more than expensive property. That's why she liked Clara and her group. They treated her like a person. That's why she would get them back, even if she had to play dumb.

"Now," the professor said, "I saw you toss the machine into a vortex. You wouldn't have sent it back to Clara, now would you?"

"Clara programmed me to destroy the time machine if ever it were clear that it would fall into the wrong hands," Misako said. Lying was a complicated human behavior, and he probably had the notion that robots were beings that had no free will. She was pretty sure he would just go with whatever she said.

"We both know that you're not telling me everything. Where did you send it? We both know the laws of robotics prevent you from lying to a human."

Misako had stopped following the laws of robotics the moment she signed up for this crazy mission. "I sent it to before the Earth was formed. The fires that forged the world should destroy it."

"Clara's a smart girl. I'll have to tell her that when I rescue her from the evil Spanish Conquistadors." He turned to his goons and said. "Take her back to home base, and pulverize her for scrap."

The two goons picked her up and dragged her away. She put up a struggle, but not too much of a struggle. She was already programming her transmitter to connect with the time travel device when it got back to 1972. She just needed to convince him to delay a while. "She'll never like you! Not now, not before you're a billionaire!"

"For once, the scrap metal makes a good point. I do have a time machine. I can go back to save her whenever I want. Let's go, boys."

The goons dragged Misako into a van that was just over the hill. Now she'd just have to hope that Pete was currently planning a cunning escape from whatever trouble he'd encountered in 1542. Of course, she wasn't sure if cunning was in Pete's dictionary.

16

Coronado tied his prisoner to a horse and rode into town at a pace that was always a step or two away from Pete's being able to keep up, letting friction do the rest. It was an adobe village like Pete had seen on a school trip to a Native American pueblo, except there were real Native Americans, and Spanish soldiers milling about. His wrists burned from the rope; his legs ached. The sun had fried his skin, and his lips were dry. He'd never really thought about how much the past sucked until he was on the ass end of it. Modern handcuffs were way more comfortable by comparison. He should know. Pete and his buddy Tito had gotten arrested when they'd attempted to toilet paper their friend's house, got the address wrong, and toilet papered a senator's house instead.

The Spanish army squatted in tents. Though from the looks of it, the officers had helped themselves to the Native Americans' dwellings. On the way through town, both the Native Americans and Spanish gave Pete the "Glad it's not me" look and gave a wide berth around the spectacle.

Pete attempted to ask for some cream for his chaffed wrists, as he was tossed into a dark adobe building with no windows. Had Pete chosen a different career that didn't rely so heavily on his wrists, he probably wouldn't have worried. Since he was a cook, the flip of the egg was all in the wrists, and what's a breakfast burrito without an egg? Pete was pushed into a corner and shackled to the wall. The door slammed, and what little light was in the room was gone.

"Hey," Pete called out to the darkness. "Hey, could you undo my wrists? I promise I won't try to escape, or anything!"

Instead of a reply, there was a wheezing cackle in the blackness.

"You Englishmen are all the same," the voice said. "You expect everyone to treat you like royalty when you are poop like the rest of us."

"I'm not English."

"So why do you speak like one?"

"My dad never taught me Spanish. He was an asshat."

"HAHA! Gear for the head and ass. I like you, boy. It's a shame Coronado will feed you to the lion."

"Isn't that what they do in Rome?"

"Where'd you think he got the idea, boy! Do you think the people of this pueblo are innkeepers? They just let anyone stay in their houses? Coronado fed their elder to the lion!"

"My friend Tito got a free night at the hotel-casino from his loyalty rewards card. I think it was at this pueblo, too, if I remember correctly. It's hard to tell without the highway—"

"Your friend won't save you, boy! Coronado has no loyalty to anyone but himself. Take me, for example. I cooked for him for him this entire expedition, and burnt the eggs just once! Yet here I am. Lion food! No loyalty—no reward—just do the job, or you die."

"Wait, you're the cook?"

"I was, but now I'm nothing, boy. Just lion food in the flesh."

Even though Pete had never been good at making plans, he was formulating one. He'd bought Star Wars tickets for the new release, and had planned to wait in line at 2 am the day before so that he could be the first person in the theater. He'd ended up being there two days late, so that by the time he woke up the next day, not only had he missed the premiere, but he'd also been ticketed on loitering charges.

However, unlike the Star Wars premiere, which depended on knowing things like the days of the week, this plan was simple. He would tell Coronado he could cook. He'd make him the best damn breakfast burrito, since he had the professor's recipe, and maybe earn the Conquistador's trust, enough to get his help looking for the others.

———

Unk hid in fear of the strange beast creature that had attacked his friend, Pete. He quivered inside a piñon tree, far from the eyes of the demon. There had been many strange things to cross his path since meeting his new friends, but nothing quite as horrifying as a man fused into the back of a horse.

Cars at least provide comfort when they swallow you whole and spit you out in a new location. The massive buildings, and flickering lights, of Pete's world were pretty. It was as if the stars from the heavens had come down to earth. Even the strange clothing they wore was amusing.

However, a man-beast hybrid was just more than Unk could take. He remembered when he was a child, the elder of his village used to do the buffalo dance. He would adorn a buffalo skull, and dance around the fire at night. The image had terrified him, and he'd have nightmares.

That's when Unk decided that laughing was way better than being afraid. He began with small pranks at first, such as squishing blueberries into water skins and turning the lips and tongue blue of all who drank. At first, the village laughed with him. It was just Unk being Unk.

He'd gotten bigger and bolder with his pranks until he'd crossed the line, and the village felt he'd angered the gods. But Unk knew that half man, half horse abominations were more an affront to the gods than some stupid prank. After a while, he had enough of living in fear.

His village did everything in fear. They prayed to the gods in fear of the rains not coming. They feared the sun would dip below the Southern sky in the winter, and never return. They greeted people from other villages with fear and disdain. Unk was sick of it. If he were anything like his village, he would have clunked Pete over the head the moment they'd met, and would have never met his best friend.

Unk knew that the time for fear of each other was over. There were truly terrifying things out in the world that were worth his actual worry, and all his village feared was nothing by comparison. They had rejected him, and now it was time for him to reject them, at least their ways. He would always love his fellow villagers at heart, but Pete was his new village now. He would get his village back.

Unk stepped out of the piñon tree, into the sun. It was the hottest part of the day. He felt the sun sucking the moisture from his body. He gritted his teeth and walked toward the last place he'd seen Pete. After a moment or two, he came across the dip in the landscape where they first had appeared. He trotted towards the center and saw the hoof tracks circle Pete's. Both went off in one direction, which was a relief. Pete was still alive. Unk could save him.

Since Unk had become an expert tracker during his exile, it would be easy to follow the trail. Before he was able to go two feet, there was a crackle overhead. Unk knew that sound. It was the sound of one of those windstorms that Clara could summon, the ones that would whisk them away to magical places.

Maybe Clara and the metal lady were on their way right now to help them! Unk could not contain his excitement and looked toward the portal. It crackled and hissed and spat out the windstorm machine. The device clunked Unk alongside the head, and he was out for the count.

––––––––––

Pete was trapped in the pitch black, for what felt like days, with only the company of a madman for conversation. He was starved and weak. The jailor that would give them a meager bread and water ration would not listen to any of Pete's attempt to convince him that he could cook. Pete also tried to use what little Spanish he knew by saying 'huevos,' and smiling. The man didn't react to Pete at all. He just shoved water and bread into his hand.

Finally, after Pete felt he was about to lose it, Coronado entered the prison cell, in his shining armor, and held a torch. Pete got to see his cellmate, and it wasn't pretty. The man had a mop of long tangled hair and a beard that hadn't been trimmed in ages. He was gaunt and weak. It was a vision of Pete's future if he didn't get out of this.

Coronado went to Pete with his torch and said, "Are you ready to talk now you English pig?"

"I'm telling you; I'm not English," Pete said.

"That's fine," Coronado said. "We will torture you until you are ready to confess. Vargas!"

A grizzled man, with a scar instead of one eye, entered the room. He had a satchel slung over his shoulder with various metal implements. He grinned when he saw his target and began setting up a workspace.

"At least it's not the lion!" the other prisoner said.

"Shut up!" Coronado slapped the guy. "Or I will feed you to my lion."

Pete eyed Vargas, while he pulled various blunt and sharp objects from his satchel, and set them up on the table. Pete gulped, and said, "OK, fine. I'll talk! I was sent here by the Queen!"

"The Queen? The King of England is Henry VIII!" Coronado said, and he squeezed Pete's neck. "He is not known for having a queen for very long. Am I right?"

Vargas laughed, as he polished a sharp three-pronged instrument.

Pete had better think of something quick. He didn't know anything about history. He knew that Sigourney Weaver had played a Spanish queen named Isabella in a movie once. The only reason he knew that was because he'd had a crush on Sigourney Weaver ever since he was a kid. She was in Ghostbusters and Aliens. She kicked ass and floated above her bed. What wasn't to like? Coronado squeezed harder, and Pete gagged, and said, "No, I'm sent by Queen Isabella. I'm one of the best English chefs in the land. She had me kidnapped so that I'd work for you."

"Why would the Holy Roman Empress send an English pig to poison me?"

What was that movie about again? Unlike some of Sigourney's other movies, that one put him to sleep. Pete had always figured that if they wanted to teach students about history, there should be more ninjas and action sequences in historical dramas. Pete had trouble paying attention without them.

Then it hit him. The movie was about Columbus. It was Columbus Day! He was pretty sure the movie was like Groundhog Day, except instead of reliving the same day over and over, Columbus went on a boat somewhere. Though Pete wasn't quite sure where. "Um—she didn't want me to poison you at all. She wanted me to celebrate Columbus Day."

"Columbus Day? That pig dog!" Coronado slammed Pete's head against the wall and began to pace. "Why would he get a day all to himself. He didn't even find any gold! I'm finding the Seven Cities of Cibola! You'd think *one* city of gold would be worth a holiday, much less seven!"

"She wants to change it to Coronado Day—"

"Really?"

"—and build a better mall!"

"You are not messing with me?"

"No sir, I'm just following orders. We'll teach that jerk-hole Columbus a lesson."

"He's dead."

"But I thought Isabella—"

"That was a different Isabella. I've had enough of your shenanigans. I will feed you to my lion!" Coronado waved his hand. Vargas packed his torture implements up, looking forlorn. Two big soldiers came into the room and began to unshackle Pete.

"No—please—" Pete cried out. The men dragged him to the front door, and he grabbed onto the frame. He pleaded for his life. "I'm a really good cook. You can chain me to the stove. You can even control the ingredients! I'll only cook what you want me to. I'm also good at working with food allergies. Speaking of which, do you think your lion has a food allergy? Humans might give him indigestion."

Coronado waved his hands, and the guards tossed Pete to the ground. The Conquistador walked up to Pete, and said, "Fine, if you are as good a cook as you say you are, then you should not mind doing a little test. I will put you up against my current cook, Vargas."

"That guy is your cook?"

"He also tortures people. It's good to have hobbies."

"OK, done! I'll have a Cook-Off."

"Not so fast. If you win, I'll let you go free, back to Isabella, and tell her I do not need a cook. I can buy my own, with all the gold I'm going to find. If you lose, Vargas can use you as the main ingredient in his next dish."

Vargas grinned a toothless smile.

"I'd better not lose, then!"

"There is one more condition. You must do it all while avoiding being bitten by my lion!"

The other prisoner spoke up. "The lion! Not the lion—That foul creature ruined my career."

"You shut up." Coronado slapped him.

"Hey, don't I get a mentor or something? Any time chefs challenge each other on reality TV, they get mentors," Pete said. He figured if he could free the prisoner who'd already encountered the lion in the past, and survived, at least well enough to be locked in a dungeon, rather than being eaten alive, maybe the guy would tell him how he'd thwarted the lion.

"What is this reality TV you speak of?" Coronado questioned.

"Um, it's English law-making—for um—The Vision of Christ. Each Cook-Off contest shall have a mentor. I choose him." Pete pointed to the prisoner.

"Sangre de Christo! This man will be your mentor." Coronado made the sign of the cross, nodded to his entourage, and they unhooked the prisoner. The man groveled at his feet and whispered his thanks.

"Come on." Pete lifted the man to his feet. "We have a lot to talk about."

"Guards!" Coronado yelled. "Prepare the Cook-Off!"

A horn blew, and the guards echoed the order throughout the village.

17

Unk woke up a few hours later with a really bad headache. He felt the patch of dried blood on the top of his head, and his lips were cracked from the heat. He felt woozy. He needed water badly, and knowing that the desert had claimed the lives of too many who'd ignored their thirst, he decided to get a drink. Unk knew the river valley well. Based on the position of the mountain, the nearest stream would be a few hours walk out of the desert.

After filling up in a stream, he dunked his head and cleared some of the blood. He turned around afterwards and looked at the windstorm device he'd collected before making his way to water. It was a strange device, with a foreign language that appeared on the screen. Unk knew the glyphs meant something, but he wasn't quite sure what. Clara was the only person smart enough to operate it. She must have been a priestess for her tribe.

He knew enough to know that it was important. Pete needed to see this object and use it to reunite them with the members of his new tribe. The only problem was that with each passing hour Pete would be dragged further and further away by the horseman. Unk could find his way back to the clearing where the horsemen's tracks began, but with each passing hour, it would be harder to follow. The winds swept away tracks in the desert. Unless it was a calm day, the trail would go cold.

That's when Unk saw smoke in the distance. There were buildings miles away on the other side of the river. They were not in his land anymore, because the place existed where no settlement had existed before. The structures were not quite of the size and grandeur of Pete's buildings. They were squat and made of sand. Either way, it would be a good place to start.

Unk set out towards the settlement. He knew he would have to watch from a distance for a while. If they were holding Pete, he couldn't just stroll into town. They would capture him too. So, Unk decided he would hunt for a couple of days of food first. He would dry some rabbit, and collect some berries.

When he'd been an exile, he'd learned the value of observation. There were a couple of different villages that had shared the area where he'd lived. Some were more distrustful than others. Before walking in to exchange pelts, he'd always watched them for a few days. The first time he'd wandered into an unknown village, they'd almost killed him, for fear he was there to steal their grain. Instead, he'd just wanted to trade for the goods he needed to survive on his own.

That life was over now. He was happy to have found a tribe where they could all work together. This thing that Pete called a 'food truck' sounded like an excellent idea. Unk had always liked cooking for people, and to think that people would give valuable things, in exchange for what Pete called the 'burrito,' was amazing.

He pictured Pete and himself always covered with furs and being given sacks of grain, just for feeding the other tribes. He wanted to have that future, so he headed towards the sand village to find his friend. Unk ended up skulking on the outskirts of the village for days before he got wind of the tournament where Pete would be fed to a lion.

————————

Pete was led out into a makeshift coliseum at the center of the village. There was a makeshift wall, held up by support beams on the outside. On the trampled earth in the inside of the circle were two fire pits. On top of the pits were two stovetops surrounded by a variety of pots and pans, prepping space, and various ingredients. There was a fence that divided the two areas, no doubt to keep out the lion from the other side.

Pete leaned on one of the 45-degree angle support beams for the wall, while he waited to enter the arena. His "mentor" glanced into the ring, and said, "It looks as though we've got some time. They're still warming the fires. My name's Javier, by the way."

"So you've been in this thing before," Pete said. "What's your secret with the lion?"

Javier shrugged, and said, "Don't get bit."

"So how do I do that?"

"You'll have to find a way to distract it," Javier said. "It's not easy. The cat is a vicious hell-beast that takes pleasure in your pain."

"You survived."

"Barely—"

A horn blew. Coronado and his entourage entered the lavish seating area at the front. There were two wings of bench seating off to the side. All the Spanish soldiers sat on the side with Vargas. They cheered and hooted wildly when Vargas walked into the arena. He waved and nodded. The man was dressed in the finest clothes.

Pete was thrust into the other side where all the Native Americans sat. One of them clapped, saw that no one else was cheering, and quieted down. The man looked familiar, but Pete couldn't place him. Either way, his cheering section looked grim and stoic. Probably, because they had seen too many of their brethren fall to the lion, Pete thought. Coronado waved his hands, and the soldiers became silent. Pete and Vargas stood at the front of the arena.

Coronado gave a speech in Spanish. Even though his language abilities weren't that good, Pete did hear a couple of choice words such as 'muerto' and 'cocinar.' 'Death' and 'cook' were all he needed, to know why the soldiers would periodically erupt with laughter from his speech.

After all the formalities were over, Coronado shot a wheel lock pistol into the air. He missed and killed his lieutenant. The Conquistador shrugged and sat to watch the Cook-Off. Vargas ran to his prep table and started throwing together ingredients.

Pete was a little slower to his station, on the account that he had been chained to the wall for the last couple of days. Pete pulled out the professor's formula from his pocket. For the most part, it was like any other day prepping for his burrito truck. He dashed between ingredients. Get the eggs ready to cook. Chop the green chile. Get a pan ready for the potatoes. It was a routine he had performed so many times before. It was like second nature to him.

He was in the flow of the moment when he noticed something important was missing. There were no tortillas! How can there be a breakfast burrito without any tortillas? Pete knew they should be in a plastic bag somewhere. Did they even have plastic back then?

He looked frantically around for the tortillas when he noticed Vargas was kneading dough. He was expected to make his own? Pete had never made a tortilla in his life! He'd always bought them in bulk from the various vendors in Albuquerque. The closest he'd ever come to fresh ones was the machine at the Frontier restaurant near campus, that would pump out warm tortillas like magic.

He panicked for a moment, and then he remembered his grandmother's house. It was a distant childhood memory. He was too young to know that his father was an asshole. He liked being with his father back then. They would go to grandmother's. There would be a wooden container on the counter with fresh, homemade tortillas.

Pete's mouth watered at the memory. He dug deeper and remembered being held to the kitchen counter by his father, while his grandmother taught Pete to make tortillas. He summoned the memory from deep within. He scooped flour and mixed in the lard. His hands were on autopilot. It was working. He was making fresh tortillas.

Then he heard the crowd chant. They called for the lion. The chant got louder and louder until it climaxed to a deafening roar. Coronado told the guards to bring in the lion, and the soldiers screamed and cheered.

Pete finished his first tortilla and tasted it. The thing was awful. It tasted like stale ramen noodle, without the flavor packet. Pete could not kid himself. He didn't know how to make tortillas. It was just his luck to be stuck in a Cook-Off before there were supermarkets. The lion might as well eat him.

The gate on his side of the arena swung open. Pete froze with fear, and wet himself. The soldiers laughed and pointed. The Native Americans nodded and talked quietly amongst themselves.

What came through the gate was not expected. It wasn't a snarling lion out of a Roman gladiator match. Nor was it the New Mexico variety, called mountain lions, that might not be as big as the African kind, but which was certainly fierce. It was a cute white cat, with black and orange patches, in a cage, on a red velvet pillow with the word 'Lion' (in Spanish) embroidered on the pillow. Even though the creature was very adorable as two soldiers paraded it on the field, the soldiers howled bloodthirsty cries, and Javier squirmed in horror.

"You didn't tell me that *Lion* was a house cat!" Pete yelled at Javier.

"They're all hell-beasts!" Javier yelled back.

"You got me worked up for nothing."

"I'm allergic to cats."

The soldiers placed the cat on Pete's table, lifted the cage off, and ran like hell out of the arena. Pete shrugged and continued to cook. Lion paraded between the ingredients on the table, purring, and rubbing his head on the various jars. Pete reached his hand out, and said, "You're not so bad, little guy. I'm sure they gave you a bad—"

As soon as Pete's hand got close, the creature casually swiped with its claws and drew blood. The soldiers hooted with laughter and pointed. Pete tried to ignore the animal at first, but it kept biting Pete. It wasn't just a soft love-bite, as when a cat wants to remind their owner of their empty bowl. It was a full-force chomp on his hand.

Lion toyed with Pete, while he tried to cook, with painful nips and scratches. Even Javier laughed, and said, "Hah! Hah! I told you! Hah! Hah!"

Pete tried every trick to get rid of the cat. He tossed some bacon, and Lion chased it, only to come back wanting to play some more. Pete would ignore it, and attempt to chop some vegetables. The cat would sit on the lettuce he was shredding and purr. Lion was a pest, and eventually Pete got so upset, he tossed the kitty away.

The cat thought it was a game, dashed back, and clamped onto Pete's leg with its chompers. The soldiers loved it, and Vargas was getting ahead. He already had meat sizzling on the grill. Coronado looked bored, but anything that wasn't a city of gold would probably bore him. Even the Native Americans were mildly amused at this point.

Pete was on his second attempt to create a tortilla when Lion swatted his arm. The cat tore a hole in his favorite shirt. It was a Metallica t-shirt from back when they all still had long hair. It was a concert his dad had taken him to when he was thirteen. Pete had never been at a concert before then. It was a badass concert. It was a shame that his dad had drunk too much, and passed out in the parking lot afterwards.

Pete slammed the dough on the table and collapsed to the ground. A stupid cat had defeated him. All his life, he'd just wanted to make burritos. Whenever it would get to be too much around the house, when his mom and dad would yell too much, he would sneak out to Golden Pride down the street, and scrape together his earnings, to buy a burrito. The employees were nice to him and would let him stay as long he wanted. Food had brought him comfort during his worst times in life. All Pete wanted to do was give other people comfort.

"Meow," Pete heard Lion mew from the table. That stupid cat! Pete stood up and saw the cat was kneading the tortilla dough. The creature purred and kneaded. It was obsessed with the dough. He petted the cat; it purred while it kneaded, and arched its back. That's when Pete had an idea. He created more dough, and the cat went to work. The cat was too busy with the dough to bother Pete.

He rushed around getting the ingredients to cook. With Lion no longer bothering him, he could get to work. He didn't need to be a good cook. He still had the professor's recipe. Pete began cooking, making eggs, potatoes, green chile, bacon, and even used some of Unk's spice. Back in the truck, he had optional ingredients like guacamole, salsa, beans, pico, and other optional flavorings for his customers. He'd make them the night before, and put them in little containers, so he could hand them out as necessary.

Pete had to choose what would be his garnish. He didn't know what Coronado liked, so he peeked over at Vargas, who was slicing tomatillos. Pete decided to go with straight salsa and gathered his sliced tomatoes. He threw two round sheets of dough onto the stove without looking. One was the one that the cat was playing with. It probably didn't matter. They didn't know anything about hygienics back then.

Once the tortillas were done, he took a taste of both, just to make sure he'd done it properly. Something strange had happened to the dough. The one he'd kneaded tasted like cardboard. The dough the cat had kneaded tasted wonderful. It elevated the tortilla beyond the mere casing of a burrito, to another plane of culinary existence.

Pete wadded some more dough and tossed it to the cat. He grabbed the current sheet the cat had made and tossed it into the fire. He put on the eggs and got together the finishing touches. He pulled the tortilla from the flame; it was perfect and smelled delicious. He tossed the ingredients together, rolled the burrito, and garnished it. He raised his hands in victory, and the horn blew.

The burrito on the plate before him was the best he'd ever made. It was a beautiful sight to see and brought a tear to Pete's eye. Lion purred and nudged Pete as if to thank him for all the fun it had had with the dough. Pete petted the cat without any severe damage.

Pete picked up the plate to present it to Coronado, and he noticed Vargas had already beaten him to it. Coronado burped and plucked the last bite from the plate. In between mouthfuls, he waved his hand and said, "Vargas—take the prisoner away; do with him what you will."

"Wait!" Pete said. "You haven't even tasted mine yet!"

"I can't help if you are too slow. I'm already done eating."

"That's not fair! If I'd known it was a race—"

Coronado cut him off, "If there is one thing I can not stand, it is a sore loser. Some people find cities of gold. Others, just a bunch of stupid pyramids. Sure, the Aztecs had some gold, but nothing like what's going to be in those cities. I just want everyone to be cool when I come back to Spain with enough riches to sink five hundred galleons. In the spirit of being cool, we'll have someone try your stupid burrito. Hector!"

"Si, mi Señor." Hector stood at attention. He was the replacement lieutenant for the one who'd died from the wheel lock pistol accident.

"Take a bite of this burrito, and tell me what you think." Coronado waved the man forward.

"Si, mi Señor," Hector said and reached over for a bite. He chewed and thought. The entire crowd was silent. Hector's eyes first looked distant. Then they lit up. His faced lifted. The man looked as if he'd just tasted heaven, then he said, "The tortilla is good, and so is the spice. The rest tastes like shit."

"That's not fair!" Pete said. "He's biased."

Pete shoved some of the burrito in his mouth and spat it out after a few bites. Hector was right. It was almost a shame to put those ingredients in such a good tortilla. The potatoes were watery, the eggs were dry and rubbery, the bacon was under-salted, and the green chile tasted almost nonexistent.

Was that what Pete's burritos had tasted like all the time? If that were the case, it was no wonder orders had increased from the fraternities during pledge week, for all the hazing rituals. All this time, Pete had thought it was students being cruel when it was him. Who was he kidding? He would never make the perfect burrito.

Pete sat on the arena floor, despondent. He didn't even try to pet Lion. The cat had taken a shine to Pete, ever since he had shown it the wonderful world of dough. Coronado got bored and waved his hand. Two guards grabbed Pete by the shoulders, and Vargas sharpened two meat cleavers with a big grin.

18

While the Spanish armies were setting up for the tournament, Unk crouched in a grove of cottonwood trees. A map of the sand village where Pete was held was etched into the dirt of the forest floor. The elders of several tribes surrounded him. They spoke in a language that was unfamiliar to him, yet much more familiar than the language of Pete and Clara. During the days Unk had scouted the town made of sand, to look for Pete, he'd met some of the Native American tribes.

Unk did what he always did with new people. He chummed around with them and played a couple of pranks here and there. After a few of the pee in the old waterskin gags, he quickly became one of the most popular guys among the tribes. Men loved him, and women wanted to be with him.

The tribes had a lot in common with Unk. They didn't like the Spanish in the sand village either. Since Unk wanted to find his friend Pete, who was captured by the Spanish, it turned out to be a mutually beneficial relationship. Since every tribal elder liked Unk, he'd had the added effect of uniting the tribes against the Spanish.

Unk's antics were just the catalyst they needed to rally together to drive the Spanish from their lands. They'd decided the perfect moment to strike out was during the sporting match Coronado held every Saturday where he executed prisoners. The tribes were expected to sit on the side of the projected loser. The wives would hide their weapons under the bleachers the night before. Then they would strike out near the end of the match when the soldiers were sloppy and drunk.

———

The guards dragged Pete to the center of the ring. The meat cleavers rang out as Vargas brushed them together. The unfortunate time traveler was shoved onto one of the prep tables. The soldiers screamed with anticipation. One of the guards gripped his arm, while Vargas raised the cleaver high into the air. Pete closed his eyes.

THWACK! Pete could feel pressure let up on his arm, and it wasn't from losing it. He sat up, and saw the guards running. Vargas lay dead, with an axe embedded in his skull. There was a roar from the sidelines. The Native Americans pulled out weapons from under the benches and flooded into the arena.

The soldiers fumbled for their muskets but were unable to load them in time for the onslaught. The groups collided; both soldier and warrior fell. Some Spanish were able to pull out their daggers in time, and axes cut others down. Pete saw a Native American man covered in furs charging towards him. Lion purred at his side.

Pete scooped up the kitty and rolled off the table. The warrior's axe came down, and almost struck him, but stopped a few inches short. He heard a familiar laugh. Underneath all the furs was Unk. His friend threw off his hood and began making fun of Pete's terror. Pete punched Unk on the shoulder and then gave him a hug.

"I never thought I'd see you again, buddy," Pete said.

Unk shrugged and remembered about the device he was carrying. He pulled it out from his cloak and handed it over. "Good work, buddy!" Pete said and looked at the device for a few seconds. He had seen Clara generate the time vortex plenty of times, and figured he could get them back. He looked at the battle raging around them. Coronado had slipped away during the fight.

"Come on; we don't want to use the portal here. I think there's a casino here in the future, and I don't want to be at a buffet anymore. Hopefully, Misako is waiting for us in '72." Pete motioned them forward and scooped up Lion, who seemed to have taken a liking to Pete.

They took the quickest route out of the besieged town. Just outside the village, there was the grove of trees that Unk had used to plan the assault. Before they'd made it halfway there, Pete heard the sound of hoofs. He craned his neck to see what was happening; Coronado was charging at them on his horse. There was a blood thirst in his eyes.

"Come on!" Pete yelled, and they ran harder. The hooves got closer and closer. The sound was right upon them when they got to the edge of the trees. Pete and Unk ducked into a dense thicket.

They heard Coronado dismount, pull out a sword, and yell, "You cannot hide forever. I will kill you, you English pig!"

Pete and Unk wove through the forest, as they heard the clink of armor behind them. If they opened the portal without enough distance between them, there was a chance that Coronado would jump through. If he made it, not only would they have altered history again, they would still be stuck with the same bloodthirsty-swordsman problem. They had no idea how to fight with a sword, much less against a guy who had probably learned from birth.

Pete was about to run out of steam from all the dashing and ducking between the cottonwood trees. Unk seemed to be doing fine; what was an all out sprint for Pete seemed to be a light jog for Unk. His caveman friend bounded through the forest with no problem.

They came across a particularly dense thicket. There were two trees growing close together, and Unk slid between the two with ease. When Pete tried to squeeze his way through, he became stuck. Coronado appeared from around a tree and saw Pete was stuck. The Conquistador charged. Unk pulled on Pete's arm.

Right as Coronado's sword was about to impale Pete, he finally popped free. Both Unk and Pete tumbled to the ground. Lion squawked when they landed on top of him. Coronado was stuck in between the two cottonwoods. His armor was too big for the gap in between the trees.

Pete and Unk didn't waste any time. They knew his army wouldn't be too far behind. Coronado was also in the process of unbuckling his armor. They scooped up the cat, ran a couple of paces away from him, and ducked behind some trees. Pete hit the button on the device, and they stepped into the vortex to 1972.

19

Pete and Unk landed in the Bosque in 1972. Lion purred and licked Pete's head. Unk reached over to touch the kitty, and it clawed him. The caveman grunted and cradled his hand.

Pete said, "Sorry about that. This cat doesn't seem to trust anyone but me." He stood up, and Lion clawed up Pete's clothes to rest on his shoulder. The trees that had once captured Coronado were now massive and squished together.

Before they were able to collect their bearings, Pete's phone rang, which was weird on two accounts, the first being that they were well before the proliferation of cell towers, and the second more simple fact that he didn't have a charger back in the 1500's.

After a few rings, he realized it wasn't his phone at all, but rather the time travel device. A command appeared on the screen that read: ANSWER Y/N. Pete hit the 'Y' button and could hear a speaker click on. There was a lot of background noise; it sounded as though the person were in transit.

"Hello?" Pete said.

"Pete?" a voice said. "It's Misako! You need to get over here and help me!"

"Where are you?" Pete asked.

"I'm being kidnapped, and will probably be dismantled for scrap metal. My kidnapper is driving down Juan Tabo at the moment. We're heading South."

"Your kidnapper is letting you tell me all this on the phone? He seems like a nice guy. Maybe we can reason with him."

"The professor doesn't know I'm talking to you. Keep in mind that I'm a robot. I can send signals out without making any noises."

"Cool; so what can we do to save you?"

"You can start by finding me. It looks as though we're pulling into an abandoned office building. Oh, crap—I have to go now. One of the robots caught me sending an outgoing signal. I'm not sure whether they tracked you—" Misako's voice cut out, and the contact disconnected.

Pete looked at the cat on his shoulder and his caveman friend. Pete wished that Clara were with them. She was super-smart and good at thinking about stuff. He was pretty lousy at plans. Before they could do anything, they needed to get out of the Bosque. Luckily, they had landed near a trail.

————

The chopper flew over Albuquerque. Golden pillars of Burrito Shacks spread throughout the landscape. Dawn was approaching the city, and there was a glow in the sky for a brief time in the morning when the city was covered by the Sandia Mountains' shadow. The professor gave Clara a phone. There was a live streaming video of her parents. They were tied to a chair, and a man with a gun paced back and forth. Tears streamed from her mother's eyes.

"You wouldn't," Clara said, a lump forming in her throat.

"I would put on the wedding dress." He shoved a wedding dress in her hands.

She motioned for him to spin around, and when he wouldn't budge, she added, "It's bad luck to see the bride beforehand on the wedding day."

He relented and turned to look out the window. Clara began to change. While she took off her clothes, she turned the volume down, then tapped a text on the phone, and sent it to Pete. Even if he were out of the service area, it would deliver it as soon as he came back. She put on the lace monstrosity and put the livestream of her parents back up.

The professor turned around and yanked the phone back. "Don't worry—you'll see them after the wedding night—provided you perform all the bridal duties."

The thought of the professor putting his hands on her made her sick. "Seems like an elaborate plan, just so you can get laid—" she said.

He cut her off. "Oh, but it's much more than that. Don't you see? This is securing our dynasty!"

"What is this? The Middle Ages? Are you trying get my hand in marriage for land?"

"No, it's bigger than that. Don't you get it? You and I are the only ones who understand time. We're the inventors of it. If we're going to pass down our legacy, it has to be us."

"First off, we didn't invent time. It was there before us. Second, are you saying this is because you want smart babies? What the bloody hell—"

"For being a good scientist, you're slow on social cues. I always liked you, from the moment I saw you. It wasn't until I saw you work

- 124 -

that I knew there had to be a reason we were put together. The world is getting stupider. It's up to smart people to breed. You were too dense to realize how perfect we were for each other."

Clara felt insulted and grossed out. The thought of breeding with that man repulsed her, not to mention that she was always good with social cues. Unlike some of the stereotypes of scientists, she could be good with people *and* science. The man was too much of an asshat to understand his position of privilege and power. She wanted her Ph.D. so badly that she would play dumb at some of his passes at her. It was hard for her to know that she could be written out of one of the biggest discoveries in her field because some jerk-face couldn't control his libido. She would have let him have it, but there was a bigger game at stake. Her parents' lives now hung in the balance of her playing nice. She stayed silent.

"Think about it—" The professor said. "With time travel, we can control everything and everyone. I don't want to see everything I built destroyed because I married some hot, dumb model, and produced spoiled kids who'd squander away my empire. Smart people need to procreate. We need to pass on our gift to the next generation."

"That's not for us to decide," Clara said. "Time travel is not just something for one person or an elite few to exploit. It's a gift for everyone. It's up to humanity to decide how to use it."

"So you just want to give all the crazy people on Earth a tool that could destroy themselves, and hope they'll do the right thing!"

"Yeah, I mean, it worked OK for the A-bomb. We've gone almost one hundred years without nuking ourselves. You give any one person too much power, and they'll bend the system to benefit themselves. They might have reasons why they're doing it for the good of humanity in the beginning, but that's the reason we have a system in the first place. Checks and balances make sure one wack job doesn't rewrite history for themself."

"I'd be careful what you say." The professor held up the livestream of her parents. "You'll come around. I know there's a brilliant person in there. Ah—it looks as though we're here."

The helicopter landed in the Albuquerque Botanical Gardens. There was a platform with floral vines crisscrossing an elaborate white arch. Chairs lined the walkway. There were even locations for news crews to set up. The asshole was going to televise it. Clara hoped Misako and Pete would get her text message soon.

Pete hopped into the back of a 1967 wagon. The car would have been old in Pete's time but had the wear of a slightly used family car. They had made it out of the Bosque and hitched a ride going east towards the mountains.

The man in the driver's seat was a bearded Santa-Claus-looking fellow. He was wearing a t-shirt and suspenders. After Unk, Pete, and his cat got into the car, the man said, "Where are you heading?"

"Um— Juan Tabo—" Pete said.

The man grunted, and then said, "Well, I don't usually pick up strangers, but since you seem like a nice fella, why don't I take you to where you want to go?"

"That'd be awesome."

"Don't use any of that hippy crap lingo around here. Have you got that?"

"No, sir. I won't, sir."

"Now, tell me, is your friend one of those—I don't know what you call it—Hare Krishnas?"

The man was referring to Unk, who still had on the Native America furs he'd taken from the past.

"Actually, I think Hare Krishnas are bald," Pete mused.

"Don't give me any lip, boy, or I'll just let you out right here," the man said, as he began to speed up.

"Maybe you should just let us out."

"What? You don't like my company! Am I not a good conversationalist?"

"Dude, you're scaring me."

"Your friend doesn't look so frightened!"

Unk chuckled, and enjoyed the ride, as the car sped past all the others along the road, weaving through traffic.

"That's because he isn't afraid of anything," Pete yelped and held Lion from flying from side to side.

"Even if I said that I was a serial killer, and you two idiots just stepped into my car!"

"He doesn't speak our language."

"Oh, I see, you're saying that he's an illegal immigrant. He just slipped into our country looking for handouts."

"No, no, he works for a living," Pete said.

"—taking American jobs!"

- 126 -

"No, he makes a spice for my burrito business, or he will when I get the thing started."

The man slammed on the breaks and screeched to a halt. Pete's face pressed into the seat in front of him. Unk clapped and wanted to go again.

"Why didn't you say so?" the man said and extended his hand. The man's whole demeanor had changed in an instant. He put on a huge warm smile and felt as friendly as apple pie. "My name's Buck. I'm a wholesaler of potatoes—good, old fashioned, Idaho Gold—fresh from the farm to the plates of your customers."

"What the hell, man!" Pete yelled. "I almost peed myself!"

Unk laughed and pointed at Pete's crotch, which was a little wet. "From the looks of it," Buck said, "you did pee yourself."

His caveman friend laughed and mimed Pete's reactions. Buck chuckled, and said, "Oh, come on, I had you going there. It was funny."

"For you, maybe," Pete said.

"What," Buck said, with a big smile, "What do you think—that it's more fortuitous that you just happen to get into the car of a serial killer, or that you're a time traveler trying to build the perfect burrito, and you just happen to meet a wholesaler of potatoes?"

"Wait," Pete said and thought about it for a moment. Pete didn't tell the guy that he was a time traveler. The man could have noticed the device he was carrying. If that were the case—It dawned on Pete. "You're the professor!"

"What? Stop that!" Buck said and swatted Pete's hand away from tugging on the Santa beard. "No, I'm just a potato wholesaler. It's just that your professor got to me first—and since I happened to be in the area, he asked me to pick you up."

Buck pulled out a gun, and continued, "The professor said he wants me to take that little device of yours, the one he used to track you with."

"What?" Pete said. "You mean my cell phone? Did he use the Find My Friend app?"

"No, the time travel device!"

The thought occurred to Pete that Buck didn't even know what a time travel device looked like. He could give him his phone, and the man wouldn't even know what he was getting. Pete pulled out his phone and leaned close, "OK," Pete said. "But don't let the professor see it, he'll know I'm giving you my phone instead of the time travel device."

Pete winced. He wished Clara were here. She was so much better at thinking on her feet than he was. He handed over the time travel device and his phone. Buck put the gun on his lap and continued to drive.

———————

Pete, Unk, and Lion were taken into an empty office building somewhere off of Juan Tabo. It looked as though it could have been a collection of doctors' offices some time in the past, but now was empty, with a For Lease sign on the front. The overgrowth of the bushes in front looked as though it had not been a business space for quite some time.

The professor's henchman opened the door. Their boss walked past them and beckoned Pete inside. He spread his hands out, and said, "Welcome to the future corporate offices of The Professor's Burrito Shack."

They stepped into an atrium with three floors of office space encasing the courtyard. The inside looked even more derelict than the outside. A typewriter lay overturned in the doorway of an office. The window was shattered in another. "I know it doesn't look like much," the professor said, "but trust me, in another 45 years, this place will look amazing."

"You stole my burrito recipe!" Pete said.

"Which *you* stole from Unk, but unlike you, my dense friend, I learned how to make the spice myself."

"Breakfast burritos are more than just spice! The eggs, the tortillas—there's artistry to it," Pete said.

"Give me a break. Americans don't give a crap about artistry in their food. They take any crap you can shove in their fat little faces, so long as it's cheap."

It pissed Pete off to hear him say that. If there were one thing that was worth getting right, it was food. Maybe before his journey through time had started, he would have settled for less—but after being shown a better way, and that something as elusive as the perfect burrito might be possible, Pete knew in his heart that he loved food. Pete realized that he was a food snob, and more importantly, he was proud to be one.

"You don't know anything! I don't know anything either, but it's more than you!" Pete said. "Did that make sense?"

The professor shook his head, and said, "Enough; now, where's Clara? You didn't leave her in the past, did you? There's no record of her as Coronado's babe. In fact, it even says he died in a Pueblo revolt. You're lucky that didn't change much about history—now, where's Clara?"

"Um—if I tell you, won't you just strand us somewhere in history again?"

"Yeah—duh."

"So why would I tell you?"

"Because I can give you a choice: you can go back to your caveman friend's time. You seemed to be getting along pretty well back then. I'm sure that if you keep your head low, and don't interact with the other tribes, you'll live out a decent life. Or, I could send you back to Los Alamos during the 1940's, where they'll imprison you as a spy, or maybe better yet, the Old West; maybe you'll get shot by Billy the Kid. There's a lot of ways to live out short, brutal lives in the past. So here's the choice: Tell me where Clara is located, and I'll let you pick your time period. Keep her from me, and it'll be dealer's choice. I'll give you some time to think about it."

The professor nodded to his robot henchmen, and they dragged Pete and Unk towards the back of the building. One of the henchmen tried to grab Lion, and the cat clawed fake skin and circuitry from the bot. "Leave it," the professor said, and they left the cat on Pete's shoulder.

They were shuffled back into the recesses of the office and shoved into a room with only a dentist's chair, and no windows. The henchmen closed the door and locked it. Pete headed towards the dentist's chair and saw that it was occupied, though not by anything recognizable as human. Misako was in pieces!

Her eyes fluttered opened, and she said, "Oh, Pete! Hi!"

"Misako," Pete said. "Why are you all C3PO from Empire?"

"Because the professor wants to use me for spare parts, but I convinced him not to, for the time being. At least, until he finds Clara."

"I'd put you back together again, but I'm not good at that kind of stuff. I'd follow the instructions on my Lego sets, but they always ended up looking nothing like the package. I guess I'm just not good at anything. I thought I'd be good at cooking, but I screwed that up too."

"Pete," Misako said. "I see no reason to panic. I'm a disembodied head at the moment, yet I think we can get through this."

"How?"

"There's still the cooking competition."

"I don't know. I screwed up so big in the past that they were going to eat me."

"Is this Pete talking, or your father?"

"What?" Pete said.

"Did you ever think that maybe the reason you can't cook an egg is not that you're a screw-up, but because your father thinks you're one?"

"My old man has always been an asshat, but he's never stopped me from achieving my dreams. Except for the time when he smashed my bass guitar when he was drunk, and the other time he pulled me out of school to drive him home from the bar. Not to mention the time he set fire to the food truck—Wait, are you saying that my father is getting in the way of my cooking?"

"I was going to say self-confidence, but yeah."

"My father doesn't control me. He's dead and—"

"—and what?" Misako said gently.

A lump formed in the back of Pete's throat. "I brought him a burrito from my food truck one morning. The rush was over; I figured I could surprise him with breakfast in bed, which is about 11 am for him. When I entered the room, he was dead. He'd had too much to drink the night before, and his heart stopped in his sleep. I never got along with my old man, but I never wanted him to die." Pete began to cry.

"I'm sorry, Pete." Misako's one arm that was sticking out from the pile of parts patted him on the back. "It's OK—Let it all out."

"I know this is going to sound stupid, but I thought somehow if I had only made the burrito better, he'd have smelled it, and woken up."

"Sometimes people tend to process things in traumatic situations in different ways. It doesn't make those thoughts true."

"So, wait—you're saying that I can't make good burritos because I haven't fully gotten over my father's death?"

"You said it, not me."

"I'm not going to let my father control me anymore. Screw you, old man!" Pete yelled at no one in particular. "I'll make my own burritos how I want to! Let's do this Cook-Off!"

"Good," Misako said. "We can start by getting out of the room."

"Good idea." Pete went over to the door, but it was locked. "Um—so how *are* we going to get out of here?"

"Easy," Misako said. "We'll time travel our way out. Most of this area was an empty field back in the forties. A few decades should do it. Besides, we're going to need to collect some ingredients throughout time. I overheard the professor's plan. He won the cooking competition by using the very best ingredients throughout time. I figure that we can do the same. However, unlike the limited capacity of a human brain, I truly do know the best places to find the ingredients we seek, because I cross-referenced everything ever written about food in the Albuquerque area, while I waited for you to save me."

"But don't you need an Internet connection?" Pete pondered.

"I downloaded it, just in case we were in a time period without WiFi."

"The news websites?"

"No, the Internet. Did you know that there are these popular movies called "Burrito Babes" where the only way to please the customer was by—."

"You really did download the entire Internet. Now as much as I'd like to see those movies—"

"All seventeen of them? I assure you the plot is quite repetitive. For example, there's a guy named Subway Mike who is known for his foot-long, who appears in five of them, who is almost indistinguishable from Jimmy the John, who's known for his—"

"Bookmark them for me. So the time travel is a good idea, but I don't have the device. The professor took it from me."

"Then we'll steal it back!"

"We're stuck in this room."

"I have lock picks in my arm. Find my right arm, and I'll walk you through how to retrieve them manually."

Pete cracked the door to the atrium area and peeked out. One of the robot guards was coming down the hallway. Pete waited for a few moments and then reached out with Misako's disembodied hand. It was attached with a metal cord to her torso. She'd instructed him how to connect it to the power cell. A stream of electricity shot forth from the rigged weapon and zapped the guard. The bot dropped to the floor and passed out.

Pete stepped outside with Lion on his shoulder. He looked from side to side and didn't see the other robot. Unk stepped out with a makeshift backpack, made from Misako's clothes, filled with her body parts. Her head stuck out of the top of the bag, looking over Unk's shoulder.

"The third door on the left," Misako said. "I'm sensing a signal coming from the device over there."

They tiptoed through the building, and Pete peeked into the window of the office three doors down. He could see all the way to a room in the back, where the professor was talking on a phone while sitting in an overstuffed leather chair. He sat behind a large oak desk, that would dwarf anyone sitting behind it. The time travel device was on the desk.

"You're going to have to go get it," Misako said.

"He's right there!" Pete retorted.

"He's distracted. It's now, or he offs us." Misako said.

Pete placed Lion in the bag carrying Misako and then turned to the doorway. He opened the door slowly, while the professor chatted on the phone. He was negotiating some sort of real estate deal. The man was buying up properties back in the '70's, when they were cheap, and would develop them in the future when they were prime locations.

Pete crawled on the floor towards the back office. At one point, he kicked a discarded binder on the floor. It made noise, and the professor looked up from his conversation. Pete ducked to the side, behind a wall. The professor went back to talking on the phone.

Pete made it to the back door leading to the man's office and noticed it was about open enough for him to squeeze through. Pete hit the door with his foot. It squeaked as it opened.

The professor glanced toward the door, and Pete scrambled to push himself against the desk. "Hang on, Jim," The professor said. Pete could hear the chair push back, and footsteps coming around the side of the desk. Pete crawled in the opposite direction, and ducked out of sight, just in time. The professor walked over to where Pete had just been and saw nothing. While the professor was inspecting the door, Pete popped up and scooped up the time travel device.

He ducked just in time and scrambled out of sight of the professor while the man walked back to his chair. Pete waited for a few tense moments, holding his breath, until he heard, "Yeah, Jim, oh, it was nothing. Now tell me more about that contract."

Pete got out of the office as fast as he could. On his way out, he saw a bag of Buck's potatoes leaning against the wall. It was near the door in the front room, and out of sight of the professor, so Pete grabbed it. One potato rolled out of the bag, hit the floor and rolled towards the office. "Who's there?" The professor asked.

Pete ran out the door, and the professor yelled for his robot guards.

"I guess we're going," Misako said. "Quick, Pete. Connect the time travel device to the port on my head."

Pete peered into a hatch that opened into the side of Misako's head. There was a cord inside. He pulled it out and connected it to the time machine. She closed her eyes and said, "I need a few more minutes to reprogram the machine, so he can't track us."

Pete glanced down the walkway. The functional robot henchmen raced towards them. Buck came from the other direction. The professor struggled to open the door, while Unk held it shut. Pete looked around for a possible distraction. He pulled the electrified arm from the makeshift backpack. He tossed Lion in one direction towards Buck and shot off a bolt of lighting at the bot.

The bot tumbled to a halt at Pete's feet, tearing up the concrete floor when its momentum came to an abrupt end. The clawing and hissing cat was enough of a distraction to Buck, to give Unk a chance to clunk the man out cold as he struggled with the cat. The professor used the distraction to push through the doorway. He was armed and pointed the gun at Pete.

He pulled the trigger as Lion bit the professor's leg, and the shot missed. Pete thwacked the professor alongside the head with the arm. Pete and Unk ran. Both Buck and the professor were waking from their dazes as Pete and Unk ran into a back room. There were no windows or rear exits; they could hear Buck coming, and the professor rebooting one of his bots.

They were in a storage room where there were extra chairs, desks, and other office equipment. Pete and Unk piled stuff in front of the door while Misako's eyes were closed as she reprogrammed the machine. Barricading the door bought them some time, as Buck was unable to open it. A few minutes later, they could hear one of the bots at the door. It pounded at the barricade, and the whole thing began to buckle. They could hear the professor rebooting the other robot.

Just as the other bot joined the fray, and the barricade began to crumble, Misako opened her eyes. Almost a second later, a time vortex appeared. They all jumped through. The robot henchmen crashed through the door and ran towards the portal. It closed just before they could make it.

20

They landed in the desert in a clump of robot parts and people. Lion seemed to travel just fine, and landed in a sitting position, licking his arm and preening himself. Once they stood up and collected themselves, Pete noticed Albuquerque below them. However, it wasn't the modern city, but just a collection of dwellings in the Old Town area. From the looks of it, they'd traveled to the Old West.

"What are we doing here?" Pete asked.

"From what I've researched, there's a farmer who produces the best eggs. Now, come on. I want to teach you how to cook an egg." Misako said.

For the next few days, Pete followed Misako's instructions on how to rebuild her, and she taught him to cook eggs. At first, the cooking lessons were slow going. The heat would be too high, and the outside would burn, while the inside was undercooked. He'd put them on too early, and the egg would get rubbery. Pete would cook at too low a temperature, and the egg would come out wrong.

Finally, after weeks of training, he plopped an egg plate in front of Misako and Unk. They were living in a house they had rented in the Old Town of Albuquerque. Misako had patches of skin that were more metal than skin. Pete had convinced the town people that she had a contagious skin condition, and people left them alone. She couldn't turn her head at all, and one arm was completely non-functional. It was the best he could do, under her supervision, and without the proper tools. She was confident in Clara's ability to take her the rest of the way.

Misako sniffed the egg and took a bite. Pete was ready for the "You're not quite there yet" look, but when that never came, Misako said, "It's great!"

Unk devoured his egg with approval and went for more. Of course, Unk liked the eggs regardless of how they were cooked and would give his seal of approval on all of Pete's creations. Pete tasted the eggs, and they were delicious.

"You're ready," Misako said. "Now, let's go collect ingredients."

Henry Luis Vega Martinez Gomez's family had been farming the land since his father's father's father's father's father, who came to the Americas mainly to avoid being tortured and killed in a Spanish prison in Barcelona. Henry, like his ancestors before him, wanted to perfect the green chile.

He had spent years toiling on the land. He'd experimented, and bred his plants to each other. Year after year, he'd rate the plants on flavor, spice, and texture. He'd take the best plants and breed them with the best ones. Every year his crop got better and better.

Finally, he had done it. He had made the perfect green chile. The beautiful pepper before him brought tears to his eyes. His life's work was finally realized.

A time vortex appeared a couple of feet from him. Pete flew out and grabbed the pepper from Henry. "Thanks, mister," Pete said and nodded. He jumped back into the time portal.

"Shit," Henry said.

Pete stood in a wheat field, threshing wheat, while Misako chopped it off the stalk with a sickle. It was blazing hot out, and the sweat poured from his head. He felt lightheaded, and said, "Are you sure this is the best way to get flour?"

"Trust me," Misako said. "This is the best wheat crop to have ever grown in the Albuquerque area.

Unk crushed the grain in a stone bowl into a fine powder.

Pete, Misako, and Unk stood in line at a Costco. It was a busy weekend, and the place was mobbed. Pete held a package of bacon.

"Are you sure?" Misako said. "My database suggests that there is this pig farmer out—"

"Trust me," Pete said. "Costco has the best bacon."

After traveling through different time periods, collecting ingredients, and learning the different ways of the burrito, Pete felt as though he were ready to be the Jedi of the food truck world. He was finally ready to take on the professor and put his skills to the test.

They entered Pete into the 1972 Albuquerque State Fair Burrito Cook-Off. They had everything they needed, from green chile to eggs, some of Unk's spice, and everything else that made a good breakfast burrito. Pete even let Lion kneed some of the dough for the tortillas so that they would be ready when he stepped into the ring.

They were in a waiting area with all the other contestants, when the professor entered the tent with Buck and his two robot pals. They also had a large container with ingredients pilfered through time. They made it a point to sit next to Pete's group.

"I wouldn't try anything, mister," Pete said and looked around at all the people. "There are too many witnesses, and I don't think that would look good for the future king of Albuquerque."

The professor shrugged, and said, "There's nothing I can do about it now. You've already entered the contest, but I'm not worried. You see, I figure that if you were a threat, you'd have Clara with you. We all know she's the brains of the operation."

"I have plenty of brains!" Pete said. "They put me in Special Ed in high school."

"So since you escaped, but *didn't* go immediately back to save Clara, then what I figure is that you *can't* save her, because she's with another time traveler, mainly me. So, if she's marrying me in the future, which happens to be in *your* past from this moment, therefore, it's already happened, and there's nothing you can do about it."

"You lost me at 'time traveler.'"

"Let me put it simply. I already won this competition in the future, or else why would you be here?"

"I wouldn't be so certain that the future is as unmalleable as you think," Misako said.

"You're right," the professor said. "It's always better to play it safe. That's why, while we were talking, I had one of my bots sneak the bacon out of your ingredients bin. What's a breakfast burrito without bacon?"

The bot tossed the bacon package on the dirt floor of the tent and stomped on it. The raw meat squished into the dirt and earth. An announcer called the contestants to the Cook-Off stage. The professor turned and waved. "Have a good competition. May the best man win."

"That jerk!" Pete seethed, as he looked at the bacon.

Misako took off running.

"Where are you going?" Pete yelled.

"There are some porta potties close to here," she yelled over her shoulder.

"You picked a fine time to go to the bathroom!" Pete called out, but she was gone.

The announcer called the contestants up again. Pete collected the ingredients and went towards the stage. Unk headed towards some bleachers, where an audience was forming.

Misako dashed through the state fair. The jacket she'd been using to conceal her robotic nature was billowing in the wind, and her hat had flown off her head. She dodged through people walking around with turkey legs, funnel cakes, and chile rellenos. She skirted around kids hitting each other with plastic swords. She almost crashed into a mother pushing a stroller.

A few foot cops saw her dashing through the park and assumed she was up to no good. They told her to slow down and chased her through the fairgrounds. Misako saw the porta potties and ran past the line of people that were waiting to use them. She pushed past an old lady about to step inside and closed the door.

She punched in the time coordinates, and not only did it suck her through the vortex, but it also sucked most of the porta potty into the future, and it imploded in front of the confused crowd. The two police officers that were chasing her finally made it to the toilets. They saw the mess that was left and turned to each other. "I guess she really needed to poop."

The contestants brought their ingredients to cooking stations up on the stage. There were a few bored audience members. A man with thick glasses, a mop of hair, and sideburns walked up to center stage. He wore a grey suit and a cowboy hat. He yelled into a microphone, "Good morning, Albuquerque. Are you ready for the Great Burrito Cook-Off of 1972?"

There were a few claps, and one person said, "Yeah!"

"Well, let's get started! But first, let's see how this all works. Each contestant will make a burrito. The winning burrito will not only win a ribbon but also get a grand prize of $5,000! Let's meet our judges. First off, we have Judy Gundy, from the Albuquerque Tribune. She's a—"

Pete tuned out the rest of the opening ceremony. He barely made it to the last cooking station at the back of the stage. The professor was in the middle and snuck a look back at Pete. They locked eyes for a moment, and Pete turned away. Pete would beat him. He just had to remember his training. However, all the training in the world wouldn't amount to anything without bacon.

Misako landed in an empty parking lot in the future. She rolled out of the way of a flood of blue water and filth that rained from the vortex where she had just landed. The porta potty came next, hit the ground, and shattered. Misako, thankful that she wasn't drenched, stood up and ran.

The fairgrounds were empty. The buildings had that weird post-apocalyptic feeling during the offseason. The only sound was that of her shoes clacking on the concrete pavement. She didn't need to run because she had a time machine to get back, but she also didn't want to take any chances.

She connected to a local cell phone tower and used the credentials she'd borrowed from Pete, to log into the network. She mapped the nearest walking directions to the closest Costco. From the distance on the map, she was glad that she was a robot.

"Ladies and gentlemen," the man in the cowboy hat said, "Start your stove tops!"

Pete clicked the gas on his burners and preheated the oven. He dove into his ingredients. He wouldn't need to start the bacon right away, so he focused on other components first. The professor pulled out all of his materials and began to prep.

Pete chopped, sliced, and diced. He went through all the vegetables and prep, and there was still no sign of Misako. Every time he glanced towards his rival, the man seemed slightly ahead. Pete put his green chiles into the oven to roast them a few minutes after the professor. The professor's cheese was already grated when Pete had just started his.

Sweat poured from Pete's brow as he toiled away at the burrito. In the audience, Unk tried to start a stadium wave, but most people just looked bored or were talking amongst themselves. Pete felt that he was lagging behind, while his opponent expertly prepared each part of the burrito.

Misako stood in line at Costco. She held a package of bacon. A lady ahead of her with a giant cart full of stuff was trying to decide on whether or not to buy an ugly dress. She told the clerk a couple of time to take it off the ticket, then to put it back on. '80's music played softly over the speakers.

Clara stood at the end of an aisle in a wedding dress. The guests had hastily assembled themselves, as the professor had bumped up the timeline. The news crews waiting off to the side swiveled their cameras to focus on her.

The organ player cued up the wedding music, and the guests rose to their feet. This sleazy-looking old man with a gold tooth named Buck walked her down the aisle. The professor stood at the altar. He was wearing a golden tux, in the same color as the Burrito Shack's golden pillars.

Clara stepped down the aisle, one foot at a time. She was slow and deliberate. There was a phone in her garter belt. It was locked into the livestream of her parents.

Pete had better think of something quick.

Pete was losing, not just on time, but because he'd also made a few critical errors along the way. He was nervous about the competition, so he'd put a tortilla on too early, and burnt the dough. He only had one left, so he had better get that one right. He broke a few of the eggs and didn't put the potatoes on soon enough.

The entire thing was turning out to be a disaster, not that it mattered much. Without bacon, his breakfast burrito would pale in comparison to the professor's, who whistled while he worked.

"Looks as though these burritos are shaping up—and remember these stoves are brought to you from Baillio's Appliances, Electronics, and Mattress Store," the announcer said to the audience, most of which had dwindled away when they'd discovered that a Cook-Off is not as exciting as the horse races. Even Unk failed to rile up the crowd, except for a little girl with pigtails. She did the wave with him and giggled.

Pete only had a slim chance of pulling this together. He glanced up to the professor and saw slices of bacon hitting a hot pan. It crackled from the grease, and the smell wafted up into the air. There was no time left. If Pete didn't get the bacon in the pan, then it was over. It didn't matter how well he made everything else.

It was nothing, without bacon.

Misako appeared in an alleyway between two buildings back in 1972. Her assumption was correct that no one would be there to have witnessed her time travel. It was a little far from the Cook-Off, but she still had some time. She stepped out of the alleyway, and right into the two police officers who had chased her to the porta potty.

She tried to step around them when one of the officers recognized her. One of the officers said, "Whoa! Whoa, Missy. I don't know what kind of disappearing act you pulled, back there at the bathrooms, but that's destruction of public property."

The other officer grabbed the package of bacon and said, "What have we here? Costco? Hey, Jose, did you ever hear of Costco?"

"Nope," the first officer said. "You?"

"Nope. Now, I don't know where you got that, but I'm pretty sure it's not yours. Here in America, we call it stealing."

The officers were about to call it in when Misako grabbed them by their collars. She flipped them over her head into the alleyway, and they both landed with a thud. She used their momentum to tumble into the alley and landed in front of them.

They both reached for their guns, and she kicked them away. She knocked their heads together, and they both went down. She grabbed the bacon back, and said, "I'm sorry; I don't have time for this."

Misako took off running through the State Fair. She ducked past tents, dove through people waiting in line for turkey legs, and even had to skirt around a large crowd that had gathered around someone performing a circus act. The chaos was closing in around her, and she was delayed by the sheer density of people in a tight space. It was as though all of Albuquerque had decided to show up on the weekend for the fair.

Once the contest tent was in sight, she pushed it double-time. She ran at an almost inhuman speed. She could see Pete in the back, struggling. All of the contestants had already started their meat. The professor's bacon looked nice and crisp. Misako dashed towards the stage, and a fair employee held his hand out, "Whoa! Whoa! Slow down!" the man said. "Where are you off to in such a hurry?"

"I have to get this to my friend. He'd dropped his bacon before the competition began," Misako smiled.

"Sorry to hear that, but once the cooking has started, there are no outside ingredients allowed," the man said.

"—but—"

"I don't make the rules. Now, why don't you go sit down, and enjoy the rest of the show? It's almost over." The man ushered her to the bleachers.

She sat next to Unk, defeated. Unk was playing with a little girl. She giggled and laughed as he made funny faces. Lion sat between Unk's legs, looking miserable because he was in a harness on a leash. Misako had an idea. She could tie the bacon package to the back of Lion and set him loose after Pete. The cat loved him, and would probably seek him out—although cats rarely did what you asked, so maybe she could convince the little girl to take it up there. The employee who stopped her either wouldn't see the girl, or Misako could be the distraction.

Misako was well into pondering all the iterations of a plan when Unk snatched the bacon package and lobbed it well over everyone's heads towards Pete. Misako turned to the employee, but he was bored, guarding the entrance to the stage. No one had noticed the bacon package flying through the air—

—including Pete—The bacon thwacked him alongside the head, and he hit the pan he had been saving for the meat. It flew off the stove and splashed grease on the stage. The other contestants looked back towards Pete. The professor even had the audacity to smile. They turned back towards their cooking.

Pete bent down to see what had hit him. It was a Costco bacon package! It had come from the heavens and saved him! Or maybe it had been Misako, in the audience. She was cheering with Unk. With the two of them acting wild, the audience got more into it.

Pete picked up the bacon package and tore it open. The pan he had warmed up for it was in the dirt. The only pan he had left was for the eggs. That's when it dawned on him—eggs cooked in bacon grease! He didn't need two pans.

Pete turned the heat on high. Once it was scorching, he threw the bacon in, and turned the heat down, just at the right moment to make the bacon extra crispy, but not burnt. He adjusted the temperature again and scooted the bacon over. He made the eggs just as Misako had taught him.

The bacon was done, although a little covered in scrambled egg, which didn't matter because it was going in a burrito anyway. He cut the strips into tiny pieces. The audience was screaming and cheering. They were going wild. The timer counting down the Cook-Off hit the one-minute mark.

That's when he could hear the chant Misako and Unk had started, "Pete! Pete! Pete! Pete!"

His burrito wasn't even stuffed yet. He took the tortilla off of the warmer, and threw it onto the plate. He stuffed the burrito with potatoes seasoned with Unk's special spice, green chile, bacon, and the rest of the fixings. The timer was counting down; the eggs were almost done. The chanting changed to, "Ten, nine, eight—"

The last bit of egg mixture solidified. Pete tossed the eggs into the burrito and rolled it into a perfect mound of mouth-watering delight. The salsa, the garnish, "Two—One—"

"Hands up!" the announcer yelled. "Hands up!"

Pete raised his hands to the sky. The burrito before him was the most beautiful thing he had ever seen. It almost brought a tear to his eye. It was the perfect burrito.

"All right, contestants! Let's do some tasting!"

The contestants brought their burritos to the judges one by one. They cut the burritos in the center, and commented on their form, before diving into their taste. One by one, contestants were eliminated. One woman's burrito leaked like a break in a sewage line when they cut it up. Another man's was so dry, it looked as though it had stayed on a gas station hot plate for five days before he'd brought it there.

When it came down to the professor's tasting, the judges cut it open, and it looked perfect inside. It looked as though it should have been in a burrito commercial. The judges gave him praise for its smell and design. They tasted it, and their taste buds squealed with delight. They gushed and complimented him. Several times, they asked if he were a professional, to which he would answer, "No, I'm a home chef."

After a few more disasters, Pete was up for his tasting. He was worried now. As much as he knew it was the best burrito in his life, he knew that it didn't matter. If the judges liked the professor's better, then it was over.

The first judge was the woman from the newspaper. She took the plate and gave him a couple of nice comments about the garnish. She didn't sound as impressed as she'd been with the professor's. She took a knife and cut the burrito in half. Pete was a little worried that it wouldn't hold its form. He'd had too many setbacks, and had had to push everything to the limit.

The burrito held. It looked just as perfect on the inside as on the outside. The judge commented, "The initial burst of steam is just delightful, and good layering."

"Thank you," Pete said.

Another male judge said, "Yes, the contrasting colors of yellow, red, and green make quite a nice aesthetic."

Pete nodded as they chattered. He sometimes wondered how many of the judges just say stuff, just to sound as though they know what they're talking about. Pete knew it boiled down to taste in the end. They each took a forkful full of the burrito.

The female judge took a bite first. She looked confused at first. Pete thought she was going to spit it out, but then her eyes lit up, "Oh, my," she said.

The other judge took his bite, "Let's see what have we here— Holy mother of God! This is amazing!"

The rest of the judges followed suit. They fought over the rest of the burrito, yanking the plate out of each other's hands. The woman from the newspaper hoarded it, while the other judges grasped at the plate.

The announcer turned to Pete, and said, "Well, shoot, it looks as though we have a winner!" The crowd erupted with cheers, and the announcer continued. "What's your name, son?"

"Pete," Pete said.

"Pete! He is the winner of the $5,000 prize!"

The crowd Unk and Misako had riled up rushed the stage. They mobbed Pete and put him upon their shoulders. The professor stormed over to the judges and yanked Pete's burrito from them. "I demand a recount. No burrito can be that good—"

The professor took a bite of Pete's burrito, and his face changed. He stood in stunned silence. Misako walked over to him and plucked his time travel device from his pocket. The crowd cheered and patted Pete on the back. The announcer dug his way through the crowd and shoved a microphone in Pete's face. "So what are you going to do next?" he said.

Pete shrugged, and said, "I'm going to start a food cart, I guess."

Clara stood at the altar. The crowd was silent, and the news cameras were pointed at her. The professor had just confirmed his wedding vows, and it was time to confirm hers. She wavered for a moment; the professor coughed and nodded towards the video feed in her garter. She looked towards the audience. They were getting uncomfortable now, and murmuring to each other. The news crews began dialing their bosses.

She looked towards the priest; he smiled and nodded. She turned to the professor and said, "I—uh—I—"

However, before she was able to say "I do," time dissolved around her. The wedding guests, the decorations, and even the priest began to shatter into millions of tiny pieces. It was as though they were in the heart of the time vortex, and the winds of time were blowing everything away. The news crews disappeared, the chairs melted into the earth, and the wedding party blew away.

Her dress morphed into her normal clothes, and the professor's tuxedo turned into the shabby outfit of a homeless man. His beard grew to cover half his chest. His hair turned grey and fell to his shoulders. His face wrinkled and gained forty years of age in one day.

Within seconds, the time vortex swirled through the landscape and changed it to a normal day at the botanical gardens. Tourists were taking pictures of a plant. A mother pushed her baby in a stroller.

The professor cocked his head, and said, "Clara! I knew I'd see you here. I don't know how I knew, but I knew that one day I would."

"Professor?" Clara said and looked him over. He had holes in his pants and socks. His jacket was dirty, and he smelled as though he hadn't showered in days.

"When I lost that burrito competition in '72, I just knew it was over. I couldn't make a burrito that good. Hell, I couldn't even get time travel right. I wouldn't have even invented it if it weren't for you."

He coughed and fell to the ground, Clara swooped in and held him; the man must have been 90 years old, too old to be living as he was. "It's OK, professor. I'm here."

"Sometimes I think I just hung on long enough to tell you—I mean this version of you—I made a point never to cross paths with our younger selves. I don't want to change anything now."

"Look at you—" Clara said.

"It isn't as bad as you think," the professor croaked. "There are plenty of hippy communes in the '70's, to take you in. It was all worth it. You see, when I tasted that burrito, Pete's burrito, I touched divinity. There's a purpose to everything. I was just a professor so that you could unlock your genius, and Pete—well, so Pete could make his burrito. I love you, Clara, but now I know there are many kinds of love—and the love I feel is more like a father's—Keep time travel safe—Don't let it corrupt anyone like me—"

The professor fell into a fit of coughing. Clara set the professor down, and stuffed her jacket under his head, as a pillow. She dug into her pockets, to call 911, but before she could dial, she saw a battered, but still beautiful, robot woman standing in front of her.

"Misako!" Clara yelled. She ran to her and hugged her. The hugging then turned to kissing.

Pete and Unk stood there, too. Pete held his hands out to get a hug, but Misako and Clara didn't come up for air. When no hug was forthcoming, Pete shrugged, and said, "I guess I'd better call the ambulance. Do you think Misako and Clara will need one too?"

Unk shrugged and petted Lion. The cat had taken a fancy to Unk, too. Pete dialed the number and chatted with Unk. "So, you're going to love working in the burrito truck. Let me tell you, working at a college is amazing. There's always beautiful women around, and the customers are great. Even though they don't tip well, students are way better customers than cranky business people. Hey, 911—yeah, I have this guy here—"

Epilogue

Pete's burrito truck was a success. The money he'd won in the '70's had been enough to renovate the cart a little, finally remove the cat urine smell, and buy a well-stocked kitchen. He could have invested the money and made millions like the professor had, but Pete didn't care about riches. He just wanted to sell burritos. Unk became Pete's roommate, and they got a two-bedroom place in the student ghetto near campus.

Unk was a hit with the women, and men loved him. He got invited to all the parties on campus and had taken well to the fast-paced life of a burrito cart. Pete saved some of the wheat and green chile he used in the competition and planted a garden. He used Lion to knead the dough. Clara had asked when he'd first showed her the operation, "Isn't that unsanitary?"

"You're cooking the tortilla, anyway," Pete replied.

With a new burrito on the menu that outshone anything else Pete could have done, his food went from the joke of the campus to the talk of the campus. Seniors would tell freshman that if there were one place they had to try, it was Pete's. Fraternities would order large batches for social occasions. Even the campus president swung by for a burrito.

Clara, on the other hand, completed her Ph.D. and was offered the professor's tenured position, when it was clear that he had disappeared the night of the lab explosion. There was no evidence to implicate Clara, and campus police assumed that he'd packed up his experiment, and left to another country that had given him a better offer. They assumed the lab fire was a way to make off with thousands of dollars of university property, without people looking too hard.

Either way, it was an easy rumor for Clara to perpetuate. While she did get publications in physics for award-winning research, it wasn't for time travel. She'd decided that humanity wasn't ready for time travel, and kept the secret in her garage that she shared with Misako.

They'd gotten married a few months after dating, and Misako went to law school. She enjoyed the prospect of practicing law that was more concerned with justice, than ratings. They'd planned a honeymoon to the future. They figured they could still time travel, and sightsee, so long as they stayed out of things.

Which was why on a nice warm March day, when Pete was cooking in the back, and Unk was keeping the patrons waiting for their burritos laughing, it was odd to hear Clara's voice. Misako and Clara pushed through the line of students. They were wearing suits without helmets, that looked like old-timey deep-sea diving suits, with accordion arms.

A skinny freshman at the front ignored the display behind him, and said, "Could I get extra green chile? What—hey!"

The student looked miffed, as Clara shoved him out of the way, and Misako glared at him. He decided not to push for his condiment and skulked away.

"Clara," Pete said and emerged from the back. "Is that you?"

"You have to come with us! Right now! Take Unk too," Clara said.

"What's happening? What are you wearing?" Pete said.

"It's about the future. We went to the future."

"Do I turn out to be some terrible burrito kingpin?"

"No, it's worse than that. There's no green chile in the future!"

"What!" Pete yelled. "A burrito without green chile! That's like—like a burrito without bacon."

"I don't have time for you to process this right now," Clara said. "We just need you to come with us."

Pete looked towards Unk, who shrugged.

"All right," Pete said. "I'll be out in a second."

He closed the shutter on his burrito cart.

Acknowledgements

Thanks go to my wife Felicia Karas for helping me flesh out my silly ideas, Andrea Beatrice Reed for her excellent editing, Jeanine Henning for her awesome cover art work, and all the folks who've supported this book.

If you've enjoyed this book, please consider leaving a review, especially if you can incorporate a cat related pun. If you want to help out, give this book to a friend, or share it on social media. The little things add up.

For free books and more, sign up for my mailing list at my website: http://aaronfrale.com

Or Follow me on Twitter @AaronFrale

Made in the USA
Columbia, SC
03 May 2017